NERILKA'S STORY
AND
THE COELURA

Also by Anne McCaffrey

DRAGONFLIGHT
DRAGONQUEST
THE WHITE DRAGON

DRAGONSONG
DRAGONSINGER: HARPER OF PERN
DRAGONDRUMS
MORETA: DRAGONLADY OF PERN

GET OFF THE UNICORN
THE SHIP WHO SANG
DECISION AT DOONA
RESTOREE
THE CRYSTAL SINGER
KILLASHANDRA

Nerilka's Story
&
The Coelura

ANNE McCAFFREY

BANTAM PRESS

NEW YORK · LONDON · TORONTO · SYDNEY · AUCKLAND

TRANSWORLD PUBLISHERS LTD
61–63 Uxbridge Road, London W5 5SA

TRANSWORLD PUBLISHERS (AUSTRALIA) PTY LTD
15–23 Helles Avenue, Moorebank NSW 2170

TRANSWORLD PUBLISHERS (NZ) LTD
Cnr Moselle and Waipareira Aves,
Henderson, Auckland

Published 1987 by Bantam Press,
a division of Transworld Publishers Ltd
The Coelura copyright © Anne McCaffrey 1983
Nerilka's Story copyright © Anne McCaffrey 1986

British Library Cataloguing in Publication Data
McCaffrey, Anne
    Nerilka's story; &, the coelura.
    I. Title
    813'.54[F]   PS3563.A255

    ISBN 0-593-01043-4

Photoset by Rowland Phototypesetting Ltd
Bury St Edmunds, Suffolk
Printed in Great Britain by
Biddles Ltd, Guildford and King's Lynn

Contents

NERILKA'S STORY
A PERN ADVENTURE

The People

Fort Hold

Nerilka	daughter of Lord Holder Tolocamp and Lady Pendra

Her brothers and sisters in order of birth:
Campen, Pendora (married), Mostar, Doral, Theskin, Silma, Nerilka, Gallen, Jess, Peth, Amilla, Mercia & Merin (twins), Kista, Gabin, Mara, Nia and Lilla

Munchaun	Nerilka's favourite uncle and Tolocamp's elder brother
Sira	aunt in charge of Weaving
Lucil	aunt in charge of Nursery
Felim	head cook
Barndy	Hold bailiff
Casmodian	main harper
Theng	guard leader
Sim	Nerilka's personal drudge

| Garben | a minor holder, Nerilka's suitor |
| Anella | Tolocamp's second wife |

Harper and Healer Halls

Masterhealer Capiam

Masterharper Tirone

Desdra	journeywoman healer studying for her mastery
Master Fortine	Capiam's second-in-command
Master Brace	Tirone's second-in-command
Macabir	healer in internment camp

High Hill Hold

Bestrum	minor holder on Fort/Ruathan border
Gana	Bestrum's lady
Pol	runnerbeast-handler
Sal	his brother
Trelbin	High Hill's healer, believed dead

Ruatha Hold

Alessan	newly confirmed Lord Holder of Ruatha
Oklina	his young sister
Tuero	journeyman harper stranded at Ruatha during the plague
Dag	Alessan's chief beasthandler
Fergal	Dag's grandson

Deefer	holder
Lord Leef	Alessan's father, deceased
Suriana	Alessan's wife, deceased, had been Nerilka's foster sister at Misty Hold

Dragonriders at Various Weyrs

Moreta	Weyrwoman of Fort, Orlith's rider
Leri	retired Weyrwoman at Fort, Holth's rider
Falga	Weyrwoman at High Reaches, Tamianth's rider
Bessera	Weyrwoman at High Reaches, Odioth's rider
Kamiana	Weyrwoman at Fort, Pelianth's rider
G'drel	bronze rider of Dorianth, Fort Weyr
B'lerion	bronze rider of Nabeth, High Reaches Weyr
Sh'gall	Weyrleader of Fort Weyr, bronze Kadith's rider
M'tani	Weyrleader of Telgar Weyr, bronze Hogarth's rider
S'peren	bronze rider of Clioth, Fort Weyr
K'lon	blue rider of Rogeth, Fort Weyr
M'barak	blue rider of Arith, Fort Weyr

Others

| Ratoshigan | Lord Holder, South Boll |
| Balfor | Beastcraftmaster elect, Keroon Hold |

Prologue

If the reader is unfamiliar with the series *The Dragon-riders of Pern*, certain confusions may occur. *Nerilka's Story* is an ancillary tale to *Moreta: Dragonlady of Pern*, told from the point of view of one of the minor characters in that novel.

To summarize the background:

Rukbat, in the Sagittarian Sector, was a golden G-type star. It had five planets, two asteroid belts, and a strange planet that it had attracted and held in recent millennia. When men first settled on Rukbat's third world and called it Pern, they had taken little notice of the strange planet swinging around its adopted primary in a wildly erratic orbit. For nearly ten years, the colonists gave the bright Red Star little thought – until the path of the wanderer brought it close to its stepsister at perihelion. When such aspects were harmonious and not distorted by conjunctions with other planets in the system, parasitic organisms indigenous to the wandering planet sought to bridge the space gap between their home and the more temperate and hospitable planet. At these times, silver Threads

11

dropped through Pern's skies, destroying anything they touched. The initial losses the colonists suffered were staggering. As a result, during the subsequent struggle to survive and combat the menace, Pern's tenuous contact with the mother planet was broken.

To control the incursions of the dreadful Threads – for the Pernese had cannibalized their transport ships early on and abandoned such technological sophistication as was irrelevant to the pastoral planet – the more resourceful men embarked on a long-term plan. The first phase involved breeding a highly specialized variety of fire-lizard, a life form indigenous to their new world. Men and women with high empathy ratings and some innate telepathic ability were trained to use and preserve the unusual animals. The dragons – named for the mythical Terran beast they resembled – had two valuable characteristics: they could instantaneously travel from one place to another, and after chewing a phosphine-bearing rock they could emit a flaming gas. Because the dragons could fly, they could intercept and char the Thread in mid-air before it reached the surface.

It took generations to develop to the fullest the potential of the dragons. The second phase of the proposed defence against the deadly incursions would take even longer. For Thread, a space-travelling mycorrhizoid spore, devoured with mindless voracity all organic matter and, once grounded, burrowed and proliferated with terrifying speed. So a symbiote of the same strain was developed to counter this parasite, and the resulting grub was introduced into the soil of the Southern Continent. It was planned that the dragons would be visible protection, charring Thread while it was still skyborne and protecting the dwellings and the livestock of the colonists. The grub-symbiote would protect vegetation by devouring what Thread managed to evade the dragons' fire.

The originators of the two-stage defence did not allow for change or for hard geological fact. The Southern Continent, though seemingly more attractive than the

12

harsher northern land, proved unstable, and the entire colony was eventually forced to seek refuge from the Threads on the continental shield rock of the north.

On the northern continent the original Fort, Fort Hold, constructed on the eastern face of the Great West Mountain Range, was soon outgrown by the colonists, and its capacious beasthold could not contain the growing numbers of dragons. Another settlement was started slightly to the north, where a great lake had formed near a cave-filled cliff. But Ruatha Hold, too, became overcrowded within a few generations.

Since the Red Star rose in the east, the people of Pern decided to establish a holding in the eastern mountains, provided a suitable cave site could be found. Only solid rock and metal which was in distressingly short supply on Pern, were impervious to the burning score of Thread.

The winged, tailed, fire-breathing dragons had by then been bred to a size that required more spacious accommodations than the cliffside holds could provide. The cave-pocked cones of extinct volcanoes, one high above the first Fort, the other in the Benden Mountains, proved to be adequate and required only a few improvements to be made habitable.

The dragons and their riders in their high places and the people in their cave holds went about their separate tasks, and each developed habits that became custom, which solidified into tradition as incontrovertible as law. And when a Fall of Thread was imminent – when the Red Star was visible at dawn through the Star Stones erected on the rim of each Weyr – the dragons and their riders mobilized to protect the people of Pern.

Then came an interval of two hundred Turns of the planet Pern around its primary – when the Red Star was at the far end of its erratic orbit, a frozen, lonely captive. No Thread fell on Pern. The inhabitants erased the signs of Thread depredation and grew crops, planted orchards, and thought of reforestation for the slopes denuded by

13

Thread. They even managed to forget that they had once been in great danger of extinction. Then, when the wandering planet returned, the Threads fell again, bringing another fifty years of attack from the skies. Once again the Pernese thanked their ancestors, now many generations removed, for providing the dragons whose fiery breath seared the falling Thread mid-air.

Dragonkind, too, had prospered during that Interval and had settled in four other locations, following the master plan of interim defence.

Recollections of Earth receded further from Pernese memories with each generation until knowledge of Mankind's origins degenerated into a myth. The significance of the Southern Hemisphere – and the Instructions formulated by the colonial defenders of dragon and grub – became garbled and lost in the more immediate struggle to survive.

By the Sixth Pass of the Red Star, a complicated sociopolitical-economic structure had been developed to deal with the recurrent evil. The six Weyrs, as the old volcanic habitations of the dragonfolk were called, pledged themselves to protect Pern, each Weyr having a geographical section of the Northern Continent literally under its wing. The rest of the population agreed to tithe support to the Weyrs since the dragonmen did not have arable land in their volcanic homes, could not afford to take time away from nurturing their dragons to learn other trades during peacetime, and could not take time away from protecting the planet during Passes.

Settlements, called holds, developed wherever natural caves were found – some, of course, more extensive or strategically placed than others. It took a strong man to exercise control over terrified people during Thread attacks; it took wise administration to conserve victuals when nothing could be safely grown; and it took extraordinary measures to control population and keep productive and healthy until such time as the menace passed.

Men with special skills in metalworking, weaving and

animal husbandry, farming, fishing and mining formed Crafthalls in each large Hold and looked to one Master-crafthall where the precepts of the Craft were taught and Craft skills were preserved and guarded from one generation to another. One Lord Holder could not deny the products of the Crafthall situated in his Hold to others, since the Crafts were deemed independent of a Hold affiliation. Each Craftmaster of a Hall owed allegiance to the Master of his particular Craft – an elected office based on proficiency in the Craft and on administrative ability. The Mastercraftsman was responsible for the output of his Halls and the distribution, fair and unprejudiced, of all Craft products on a planetary rather than a parochial basis.

Certain rights and privileges accrued to different Leaders of Holds and Masters of Crafts and, naturally, to the dragonriders whom all Pern looked to for protection during the Threadfalls.

It was within the Weyrs that the greatest social revolution took place, for the needs of the dragons took priority over all other considerations. Of the dragons, the gold and green were female, the bronze, brown and blue, male. Of the female dragons, only the golden were fertile; the greens were rendered sterile by the chewing of firestone, which was as well since the sexual proclivities of the small greens would soon have resulted in overpopulation. They were the most agile, however, and invaluable as fighters of Thread, fearless and aggressive. But the price of fertility was inconvenience, and riders of queen dragons carried flamethrowers to char Thread. The blue males were sturdier than their smaller sisters, while the browns and bronzes had the staying power for long, arduous battles against Thread. In theory, the great golden fertile queens were mated with whichever dragon could catch them in their strenuous mating flights. Generally speaking, the bronzes did the honour. Consequently, the rider of the bronze dragon who flew the senior queen of a Weyr became its Leader and had charge of the fighting Wings during a Pass. The rider of the senior queen dragon, however, held the most responsibility for the Weyr during and after a Pass, when it was the Weyrwoman's job to nurture and preserve the dragons, to sustain and improve the Weyr and all its folk. A strong Weyrwoman was as essential to the survival of the Weyr as dragons were to the survival of Pern.

To her fell the task of supplying the Weyr, fostering its children, and searching for likely candidates from Hall and Hold to pair with the newly hatched dragons. As life in the Weyrs was not only prestigious but easier for women and men alike, Hold and Hall were proud to have their children taken on Search, and boasted of the illustrious members of the bloodline who had become dragonriders.

Now, in the year or Turn of their reckoning 1541, when the Sixth Pass of the Red Star is nearly over, the inhabitants, Lord Holders, Craftmasters and the Weyrs face a new peril, which threatens them as surely as does Thread.

Chapter One

3.11.1553 Interval

I AM NOT A HARPER, so do not expect the polished tale. This is a personal history, though, and as accurate as memory can make it: my memory, so the perceptions will be one-sided. No one can challenge the fact that I have lived through a momentous time in Pern's history, a tragic time. I survived the Great Plague, though my heart still grieves for those lost to its virulence, and ever will.

I have, I think, finally adjusted my thinking to a positive attitude towards death. Not even the most abject self-recriminations will breathe life back into the dead long enough to give absolution to the living. Like many another, what I grieve for is what I did *not* do or say to my sisters, now beyond speech or sight or the receipt of my charitable farewell on that day which was the last I saw them.

On that balmy morning, when my father, Lord Tolocamp, my mother, Lady Pendra, and four of my younger sisters set off on their journey to Ruatha Hold and its Gather four days hence, I did not bid them farewell and safe journey. Until common sense reasserted itself, I did, I admit, worry that my lack of charity on that occasion caused their misadventure. But there were plenty of well-wishers that morning, and surely my brother Cam-

17

pen's exhortations would have been a more powerful farewell than any grudgingly given sentiment of mine. For he, at long last, had been left in charge of Fort Hold during my father's absence and he meant to make the most of opportunity. Campen is a fine fellow, despite a lack of any vestige of humour and little sensitivity. There is not a devious bone in his body. As his entire plan was to amaze my father with his industry and efficiency in managing the Hold, it also required my parents' safe return. I could have told poor Campen that all the approval he was likely to receive was a grunt from Father, who would have expected industry and efficiency from his son and heir. With the entire guard complement of Fort Hold, all the cottagers, and the Harper Hall apprentices adding their exuberant presences to the send-off, there were sufficient good wishes to have pleased any wayfarer. No one would have noticed my defection. Except, perhaps, my sharp-eyed sister Amilla, who missed nothing that she might use to her advantage at a later date.

In truth, while I certainly wished them no harm, since Threadfall had been endured the day before with no infestations to ravage the winter fields, I couldn't have wished them merry on their way. For I had been left behind on purpose, and it had been hard indeed to listen to my sisters' prattling about their vain hopes for conquests at the Ruatha Gather and know that the festivities would not include me.

To be excluded in such a peremptory fashion, a flick of my sire's hand to strike me from the travel list, was another insensitive act of judgement. Typical of him when human feelings are concerned – at least typical of his attitudes and judgements until he came back from Ruatha and immured himself in his apartments all those long weeks.

There was no real reason to have excluded me. One more traveller would have made no difference to any of my father's arrangements or discommoded the expedition. Even when I approached my mother and pleaded with her, reminding her that I had undertaken all the disagreeable tasks allotted us girls in the hope of attending Alessan's first Gather, she had been unresponsive. In the throes of that cruel disappointment, I know I lost my case when I blurted out that I had, after all, been fostered with Suriana, Alessan's wife, dead of an unfortunate fall from her wild runnerbeast.

'Then, Lord Alessan will scarcely wish to see your face and be reminded of his loss on such an occasion.'

'He has never seen my face,' I had protested. 'But Suriana was my friend. You know that she wrote me many letters from Ruatha. Had she lived to become Lady Holder, I would have been her guest. I know it.'

'She is a full Turn in her grave, Nerilka,' my mother had reminded me in her coolest voice. 'Lord Alessan must choose a new bride.'

'You cannot possibly think that my sisters have the slightest chance of attracting Alessan's attention . . .,' I began.

'Have some pride, Nerilka. If not for yourself, for your Bloodline,' my mother had replied angrily. 'Fort is the first Hold, and there isn't a family on Pern that—'

'Wants any of the ugly Fort daughters of this generation. Too bad you married Silma off so quickly. She was the only pretty one of the lot of us.'

'Nerilka! I'm shocked! If you were younger, I'd. . . .'

Even holding herself erect in anger, Mother still had to look up at me – an attitude which did not endear me further in her eyes.

'Since I'm not, I suppose I shall have to supervise the drudges' bathing once again.'

I took a savage satisfaction from the expression on her face, for that had obviously been the very thought in her head for discipline.

'At this time of the cold season, they always benefit from warm water and soapsand. And when you've done that you will clear the snake-traps on the lowest level!'

19

She had waggled her finger under my nose. 'I find that lately your attitude leaves much to be desired in a daughter, Nerilka. You are to study a more congenial manner for my return or, I warn you, you will find your privileges curtailed and your duties increased. If you will not abide my authority, I will have no option but to apply to your father for disciplinary action.' She dismissed me then, her face still ruddy with controlled anger at my impertinence.

I left her apartments with my head high, but the threat of applying to my father's judgement was not one I wished to challenge. His hand weighed as heavy on the oldest and biggest of us as it did on the youngest.

When I had had a chance to review that interview with my mother, as I ruthlessly sent the drudges into the warm pools and sanded the backs of those whose ablutions were not energetic enough to suit my frame of mind, I regretted my hasty words on several counts. I had probably prejudiced my chance of getting to another Gather for the entire Turn, and I had unnecessarily wounded my mother.

It could not be considered her fault that her daughters were plain. She was a handsome enough woman even now in her fiftieth Turn and despite almost continuous pregnancies which had resulted in nineteen living offspring. Lord Tolocamp was considered a fine-looking man, too, tall and vigorous, certainly virile, for the Fort Hold Horde, as the harper apprentices had nicknamed us, were not his only issue. What galled me excessively was that most of my half-blood half-sisters were far prettier than any of the full-blood, with the exception of Silma, my next-oldest sister.

Half or full blood, we were all tall and sturdy, an adjective more complimentary to boys than to girls, but there it was. I might be a trifle hasty, for my youngest sister, Lilla, at ten Turns had daintier features than we other girls and might well improve. It was positively wasteful that Campen, Mostar, Doral, Theskin, Gallen and Jess should have black, thick eyelashes where ours were sparse; huge dark eyes while ours were lighter-coloured, almost washy; straight fine noses while no one could call mine anything but a beak. They had masses of curly hair. We girls had thick hair; mine reached below my waist when unplaited and was remorselessly black, but it made my skin look sallow. My nearest sisters were cursed with mid-brown hair that no herb could brighten. The injustice of our heritage was catastrophic, for plain males would still marry well, now that the Pass was ending and Fort's Holder was extending his settlements. But there would be no husbands for plain females.

I had long since discarded the romantic notions of all young girls, or even the hope that my father's position would acquire for me what appearance could not, but I did like to travel. I adored the bustle and uninhibited atmosphere of a Gather. I would so love to have gone to Alessan's first Gather as Lord Holder of Ruatha. I wanted to see, from whatever distance, the man who had captured the love and adoration of Suriana of Misty Hold – Suriana, whose parents had fostered me; Suriana, my dearest friend, who had been effortlessly all that I was not and who had shared the wealth of her friendship unstintingly with me. Alessan could not have grieved more than I for her death, for that event had taken from my life the one life I had valued above my own. To say that part of me had died with Suriana was no exaggeration. We had understood each other as effortlessly as if we had been dragon and rider, would often laugh as one, uttered the observation the other had been about to make, could instantly fathom each other's mood, and shared the same cycle to the minute no matter what distance separated us.

In those happy Turns at Misty Hold, I had even managed to appear prettier in a contentment reflecting Suriana's vividness. Certainly I was braver in her company, urging my runnerbeast after hers on the most dangerous of trails. And I was able to sail in the fiercest wind in the little sloop we took upon the river and sea. Suriana had other attainments, too. She had the sweetest light soprano to which my alto was always in tune. In Fort, my voice goes flat. She could sketch a scene in bold sure strokes; her embroidery was so finely stitched that her mother never feared to give her the gossamer fabrics, and with her to advise me quietly my stitches improved to the point where later my mother gave me grudging compliments. In one talent only did I surpass Suriana, but not even my healing arts could have mended her broken back. Nor could I, the daughter of Fort Hold, enter the Healer Hall for training. Not when my skills could be employed, free-marked, in the murky stillrooms of Fort Hold.

Now I am appalled at the heedless, uncharitable girl I was that day, unable to swallow disappointment and pride to bid her luckier sisters farewell. For it proved that their luck had run out when they were chosen to attend Ruatha's Gather. But who could have foreseen that, much less the plague, on the bright cold-season day?

We had heard tell of the strange beast rescued by seaholders, for my father had insisted that all his children understand drummer codes. Living so close to the Harper Hall, there was little we did not know of major events occurring across the Northern Continent. Oddly, we were not supposed to talk about the drum messages we heard, lest the information that we could not avoid understanding be indiscreetly repeated. So we all knew about the discovery of the unusual feline at Keroon. It is not surprising, then, that I failed to connect the significance of that message with the later one requiring Master Capian to diagnose a strange disease afflicting those at Igen. But I anticipate.

And so my parents and my four sisters – Amilla, Mercia, Merin and Kista – started on their journey through the northern portion of our Hold, where Father meant to check on several holders, to the fateful Ruatha Gather. I who felt she deserved to go remained at home.

Fortunately, I could also remain out of Campen's way, for I was certain he would have special duties for me to perform that would ensure our father's approbation of him. Campen adored delegating duty and thus managed to avoid its tedium, saving his energies to criticize results and expound weighty advices. He is much like our father. Indeed, when Father dies, there will be no skip in the smooth operation of Fort Hold and likely no change ever in the duty roster for me, Nerilka.

The gathering of herbs, roots and other medicinal plants was a frequent occupation for myself and my sisters, and this duty took precedence over any Campen might have had for me that day. What Campen never twigged was that one did not gather medicinal plants in the cold season, but no one was likely to tell on me. I elected to take Lilla, Nia, Mara and Gaby with me on my so-called expedition. We did return with early cress and wild onion, and Gaby surprised himself by bringing down a wild wherry with a well-thrown lance. The obvious rewards of our afternoon forced commendation from Campen, who spent the evening meal complaining about the fecklessness of drudges who worked well only under supervision. This was such a frequent complaint of our father's that I raised my eyes from the leg bone I was gnawing to be sure that it was Campen who had spoken.

I do not now recall with what occupation I passed the next few days. Nothing memorable occurred – excepting the summons for Master Capiam, which I heard and so totally disregarded. But knowing would have changed nothing. The fifth day dawned bright and clear, and I had recovered enough from my disappointment by then to hope that the weather at Ruatha was as clement. I knew that my sisters stood no chance of attracting Alessan but, with so many gathering, perhaps some other family might meet my father's requirements for his daughters, and they'd make suitable matches. Particularly now that the Pass was nearly over and Holders could plan expansions. Lord Tolocamp was not the only one to wish to extend his holdings and increase his arable land. If only my father would not be quite so particular in his standard for alliances.

There had been one offer for me, I'm pleased to say. I should not have minded starting a new hold, even if it had meant chipping it out of the cliffside, for I should have been my own mistress. Garben came from the Tillek Bloodline, respectable enough in its lateral descent. I even liked the man, but he and his prospects had not met Father's requirements. Although Garben had flattered me by returning two Turns in a row to repeat his offer – each time with the report of yet another chamber completed in his modest hold – my father had turned him off. Had my opinion been sought, I would have accepted. Amilla had unkindly remarked that I would have accepted anything at that point. She was quite correct, but only because I liked Garben anyway. He was half a head taller than I. That had been five Turns ago.

Suriana had known my situation and my disappointments and had repeatedly expressed the hope that she could talk Lord Leef into permitting me to make an extended visit with her at Ruatha. She was certain that once she was pregnant he would accede to her request. But Suriana had died, and even that glimmer of hope had been dashed, even as she had been dashed to the ground by the untrained young runner she had been riding. Racing, more likely, I often thought in my bitterest moods. She had confided in me that Alessan had managed to breed some startlingly agile runners when his father had ordered him to produce a sturdier, multi-purpose strain. I had only the details that were made public: Suriana had broken her back while riding, and had died without regaining consciousness despite all that the hastily summoned Masterhealer could do. Master Capiam, who was generally willing to discuss medical matters with me, since he knew me to be as competent as my rank allowed me to be, had been markedly silent about the tragedy.

Chapter Two

3.11.43 – 1541

HEARTBREAKINGLY ENOUGH, the new Ruathan tragedy began at precisely the same hour in which I had learned of Suriana's death, as the Harper Hall's drum tower vibrated with Capiam's quarantine command. I was measuring spices for the kitchen warder, and only the sternest control kept my hand from trembling and spilling the expensive spice. Exerting the same control, for the warder did not understand drum code and I wished an edible dinner that night, I finished measuring his requirements, carefully closed the jar, placed it exactly in its habitual spot, and locked the cabinet. The drum message was being repeated for emphasis by the time I had reached the upper level of the Hold proper, but the second message differed in no particular from the first. I could hear Campen bellowing for explanations from his office as I left the Hold.

Fortunately, so many other people were racing towards the Harper Hall that my indecorous haste went unnoticed. The courtyard of the Hall was filled with anxious apprentices and journeymen, harper and healer. There has always been excellent discipline in the two Crafts, so there was no panic, though some anxiety was evident and many questions circulated.

Yes, there had been calls for Master Capiam from

more than just Keroon Beasthold and Igen Sea Hold. Telgar had asked for his presence and counsel; it was rumoured he had been taken dragonback to Ista Gather and from there to South Boll at Lord Ratoshigan's express orders, conveyed by no less than Sh'gall, the Fort Weyrleader, on bronze Kadith.

The moment Master Fortine, accompanied by Journeywoman Desdra of the Healer Hall and Masters Brace and Dunegrine of the Harper Hall, appeared on the broad stairs, all fell silent.

'You are naturally anxious about the drum message,' Master Fortine began, clearing his throat ostentatiously. He is a good theoretical healer, but has none of the ease that marks the Masterhealer Capiam. Master Fortine raised his voice to an unnecessarily loud, high pitch. 'You must realize that Master Capiam would not invoke such emergency procedures without due cause. Would all harpers or healers who attended either Gather present themselves immediately to Journeywoman Desdra in the Small Hall? I will address all healers immediately in the Main Hall, if you would be so kind as to assemble there. Master Brace. . . .'

Master Brace stepped forward, adjusting his belt and clearing his own throat. 'Master Tirone is from the Hall mediating that dispute in the mines. In accordance with custom, as Senior Master, I assume his authority in this crisis until he has returned to the Hall.'

'Hoping that Master Tirone is either caught in the quarantine or dies of the disease . . .,' I heard someone mutter nearby. He was immediately shushed by his neighbours, so there would have been no point in my turning to catch out the dissident even if the matter had concerned me more acutely.

Before acceding to the rank of Masterharper, Tirone had once been the tutor to Lord Tolocamp's children, so I knew the man well. He had his faults, but to listen to his rich mellow voice had always been a pleasure no matter what message his words were trying to implant in dull or

26

uninterested minds. A man was never voted to be Master of his Crafthall unless he had a more than glorious baritone voice to recommend him to his fellow Masters. I have heard it said by the disaffected that the only time Tirone has lost a mediation was when he had laryngitis; otherwise, he talked his opponents into surrendering to his decisions.

Naturally the diplomatic Masterharper would take great pains not to offend the Fort Lord Holder despite Craft autonomy, so I had never witnessed that sort of pertinacity in Master Tirone.

What struck me as odd in this moment was that Master Brace should make such an announcement at all – and that Desdra and Fortine represented the healers. Where was Master Capiam? It was totally unlike him to delegate an invidious task. As harpers and healers began to file into the two assembly-points, I slipped away from the Hall, not much wiser and with much to worry about.

My lady mother, my four sisters, and my father were now immured at Ruatha. Unworthy, I thought that was another reason why they ought to have taken me. My demise would have been no loss. And I could have been of considerable use as a nurse, really my only talent and mainly unused outside the family. I remonstrated with myself for such reflections, and purposefully turned my steps to the lower level of the Hold, where the storerooms were situated.

If this disease had required quarantine, I could occupy myself profitably by checking over supplies. While the Healer Hall had viable stocks of most herbs and medicines, most Holds and Halls were expected to supply their own needs according to their individual requirements. But this situation might require uncommon herbal remedies not normally laid by in sufficient quantity. Campen spotted me, however, and came charging over, huffling as he did when agitated. 'Rill, what's abroad? Did I hear quarantine? Does that mean Father is stuck at Ruatha? What do we do now?' He recalled that if he was acting Lord Holder he ought not to be requesting advice from any lesser entities, especially his sister. He cleared his throat noisily and poked his chest forward, assuming a stern expression that I found ludicrous. 'Have we sufficient fresh herbs for our people?'

'Indeed we do.'

'Don't be flippant, Rill. Not at a time like this.' He frowned ponderously at me.

'I'm on my way to assess the situation, brother, but I can say without fear of contradiction that our supplies will prove more than adequate for the present emergency.'

'Very good, but be sure to give me a written report of supplies on hand.' He patted my shoulder as he would his favourite canine and bustled off, huffling as he went. To my jaundiced eye, he appeared unsure as to what he should be doing in this catastrophe.

Sometimes I am appalled at the waste in our storerooms. In spring, summer and autumn, we gather, preserve, salt, dry, pickle and store more food than ever Fort Hold could need. Each Turn, despite Mother's conscientious efforts, the oldest is not used first, and gradually the backlog grows. The tunnel snakes and insects take care of that in the darker recesses of the supply caves. We girls often make judicious withdrawals to be smuggled out to needy families as neither Father nor Mother condones charity, even when the harvests have failed through no fault of the holder. Father and Mother are always saying that it is their ancient duty to supply the entire Hold in time of crisis, but somehow they have never defined 'crisis'. And we keep increasing the unused and unusable stores.

Of course, herbs, properly dried and stored, keep their efficacy for many Turns. The shelves of neat bags and bound stalks, the jars of seeds and salves bulged. Sweatroot, featherfern, all the febrifuges that had been traditional remedies since Records began. Comfrey, aconite, thymus, hissop, ezob: I touched each in turn, knowing we had it in such quantities that Fort Hold could treat every one of the nearly ten thousand inhabitants if

28

necessary. Fellis had been a bumper crop this Turn. Had the land known its future needs? Aconite, too, was in generous supply.

Much relieved by such husbandry, I was about to quit the storeroom when I saw the shelves on which the Hold's medicinal Records were kept – the recipes for compound mixtures and preparations as well as the notations of whichever person dispensed herb, drug and tonic.

I opened the glowbasket above the reading-table and wrestled with the stack to remove the oldest of the Records from the bottom shelf. Perhaps this illness had occurred before in the many long Turns since the Crossing. It was dusty, and pieces of the cover flaked away in my hand. If Mother's assiduous housekeeping had not required it to be dusted off, it was unlikely she would notice the damage. The tome stank with antiquity as I opened it, carefully, not wishing to desecrate it any more than absolutely necessary. I ought to have saved myself the trouble – the ink had faded, leaving only linear splotches on the hide that looked like freckles. I wondered why we bothered to store them any more. But I could just imagine Mother's reaction if I suggested disposing of these ancestral artefacts.

I compromised by going back to the tome still legibly labelled *Fifth Pass*.

What boring diarists were my ancestors! I was heartily relieved when Sim came to tell me that the head cook earnestly desired my presence. Well, with Mother away, he was likely to apply to me. I held Sim, who was, in any case, not at all eager to return to his labours in the scullery, and quickly penned a note to Journeywoman Desdra, suggesting that Fort Hold's apothecary supplies were at her disposal. I would follow that up as soon as I could, for I doubted that I would be permitted such generosity once Mother had returned to take over the storeroom keys.

I think that was the first moment in which it occurred to me that Lady Pendra would be as vulnerable to this disease as anyone else. A pang of fear or anxiety paralysed my hand over the script until Sim's throat-clearing roused me. I smiled reassuringly at him. Sim didn't need to be burdened with my silly fears.

'Take this to the Healer Hall. Give it into the hand of Journeywoman Desdra only! Understand? Do not just hand it over to the nearest body in healer colours.'

Sim bobbed his head up and down, smiling his vapid smile and murmuring reassurances.

I dealt with the cook, who had just been informed by my brother to prepare for an unspecified quantity of guests. He was at a loss to know what to do, as the evening meal was already being prepared.

'Soup, of course – one of your excellent hearty meat soups, Felim, and a dozen or so of the wherries from the last hunt. They will have hung long enough to be used. Excellent as cold meat, the way you have with seasoning them. More roots, for they, too, can be reheated taste-fully. And cheese. We've plenty of cheese.'

'For how many?' Felim was too conscientious for his own good. He had been so often chastised by my mother for 'wastefulness' that his only defence was showing her the records of how many ate at which meal and what was served them.

'I'll discover that, Felim.'

Campen, it appeared, was certain that every nearby holder would be coming to ask his advice about the present emergency, and thus Fort Hold must be prepared to feast the multitude. But the drum message had un-equivocally specified a quarantine situation, and I pointed out that the holders, no matter how worried, would be unlikely to disobey that stricture. Those in the home farms might come, since, in effect, they considered them-selves part of the main Hold. I forbore to mention that most of these knew a good deal more about managing themselves than did Campen. Still I did not wish to depress him.

I returned to Felim and advised him to increase the portions only by a quarter but to make up additional klah, get a new cheese and more biscuits. Checking the wine stores, I saw there was sufficient in the tuns already broached.

I then went up to the dayroom on the second storey; the aunts and other dependants were already aware of the drum reports and highly agitated. I organized them to ready what empty rooms remained into infirmaries. Stuffing clean cases with straw for makeshift pallets would not be too arduous, and they'd feel better for doing something. I caught Uncle Munchaun's eye and we managed to get out into the corridor without being followed.

Munchaun was the oldest of my father's living brothers and my favourite among the pensioners. Until he had been injured in a climbing fall, he had led all hunting parties. Hc had such great understanding of human frailties, such humour, such humility, that I always wondered how my father could have been chosen to Hold, when Munchaun was so much the better human being.

'I saw you coming from the Hall. What's the verdict?'

'Capiam is now a victim of the disease and Desdra tells the healers to treat the symptoms.'

He raised his finely curved eyebrows, a wry grin on his face. 'So they don't know what they're dealing with, eh?' When I shook my head, he nodded. 'I'll start looking through the Records. They must be good for something besides keeping us elderly supernumeraries occupied.'

I wanted to deny his self-deprecation, but he smiled knowingly at me and my protestation would have fallen on deaf ears.

That evening, more of the minor holders came than I had anticipated, as well as all the Crafthall Masters, excepting the Harper and Healer Halls, of course. We had ample for them, and they talked well into the night, discussing contingencies and how to shift supplies from hold to hold without breaking the quarantine.

I poured a last round of klah, though I think only Campen drank any, and retired to my room, where I read the old Record as long as I could keep my eyes open.

31

Chapter Three

3.12.43

WHEN I HEARD THE DRUMS, I jumped out of my bed and ran into the corridor where I could distinguish their pulse. The message was terrifying. Before its echoes had died, another came in from the south: Ratoshigan demanding assistance from the Healer Hall. It was very early indeed for the drums to be speaking. I left my door open as I hastily donned a work tunic and trousers and belted on the heavy ring of Hold keys. I put on boots, too, for the soft house-shoes were no protection against the cold stone floors of the lower level, or the roads without.

The drums banged on with more casualties reported at Telgar, Ista, Igen and South Boll, and more requests for reassurance from distant Holds and Healer Halls. There were volunteers, which was heartening, and offers of assistance from Benden, Lemos, Bitra, Tillek and High Reaches, places so far untouched by the catastrophe. I found that encouraging, and worthy of the spirit of Pern.

I was halfway across the Field when the first of the coded reports came in from Telgar Weyr: there were dead riders and, because of their deaths, dragon suicides. Passing field-workers on their way to the beastholds, I carefully controlled my agitation, nodding and smiling but hastening so that no one would be brash enough to stop me. Or perhaps they did not wish to learn more bad news on top of yesterday's. Hard on the echoes of Telgar's grim news, Ista began citing its report.

Why I had thought that dragonriders would be immune from this disease I do not know, except that they seemed so invulnerable astride their great beasts, seemingly untouched by the ravages of Thread – though I knew well enough that dragons and riders were often badly scored – and impervious to other minor ailments and anxieties that were visited on lesser folk. Then I recalled that dragonriders often flitted from one Gather to another, and there had been two Gathers on the same day, Ista as well as Ruatha, to lure them from their mountain homes. Two – and plague well advanced in both! Yet Ista was halfway east. How could the disease spring up so quickly in two so distant places?

I hurried on and entered the Harper Hall Court. Everyone here was already up, half of them holding runnerbeasts, saddled and burdened for long trips, their tack in healer colours. Above us the drums continued their grim beatings. From Healer Hall to Hold and Weyr, the messages were sent by Master Fortine. Where, then, was Master Capiam?

Desdra swung down the shallow steps of the Hall, saddlebags draped on each shoulder and weighing down her hands. Behind her, two more apprentices as laden as she hurried by. The woman looked as if she had not slept, and her face, usually so bland and composed, was etched with strain and impatience, and heavy with anxiety. I edged around the court, hoping to converge on her path as she began to distribute the saddlebags to the mounted men and women.

'No, no change,' I heard her say to a journeyman. 'The disease must run its course with Capiam as with anyone else. Use these remedies as symptoms warrant. That is the only advice I have now. Listen to the drums. We'll use the emergency codes. Do not send open messages at any time.'

She stepped back as the healers urged their runners out of the court, and I had a chance to approach her.

'Journeywoman Desdra.'

She swung towards me, not identifying me even as one of the Fort Horde.

'I am Nerilka. If the Hall's supplies are drained by the demand, please come to me' – I emphasized that point by touching hand to chest – 'for we've enough to physic half the planet.'

'Now, there is no need for concern, Lady Nerilka,' she began, mustering a reassuring expression.

'Nonsense.' I spoke more sharply than I intended, and then she did look at me and see me. 'I know every drum code but the Masterharper's, and can guess at that. He's apparently on the mountain road home.' I had her full attention now. 'When you need more supplies, ask for me at the Hold. Or if you need another nurse. . . .'

Someone called urgently to her, and with a quick nod of apology to me she walked off. Then the eastern drums began a fresh dispatch of bad news from Keroon. I walked back with the knowledge that hundreds were dying in that tragic Hold, and that four smaller mountain holds did not answer their drumroll.

I was halfway across the Field when I heard the unmistakable sound of a dragon trumpeting. A chill hand clutched at my innards. What could a dragon be doing at Fort Hold – now? I picked up my skirts and ran back to the Hall. The massive Hold door was wide open, and Campen stood on the top step, his arms half-raised in astonished disbelief. A small group of anxious Crafthall Masters and two of the nearer minor holders were grouped below him on the steps; all now turned away from Campen and towards the blue dragon who dominated the courtyard. I remember thinking that my brother was a trifle off-colour. Then all else was forgotten as, incredulous, I watched my father striding up the steps, shoving holder and Craftmaster aside.

'There is a quarantine! There is death stalking the land. Did you not hear the message? Are you all deaf that you gather in such numbers? Out! Out! To your homes! Do not quit them for any reasons! Out! Out!'

He shoved the nearest holder down the steps, towards the runnerbeasts which the drudges were only just leading to the stablehold. Two Craftmasters stumbled into each other in order to avoid his flailing arms.

In moments, the courtyard was clear of its visitors, the dust of the precipitous departures already settling on the road.

The blue dragon trumpeted again, adding his own impetus to the scrambling retreat of holder and Master. Then he leapt skywards, going *between* before he had cleared the Harper Hall tower.

Father turned on us all, for my brothers had come to investigate the unexpected arrival of a dragon.

'Have you run mad to assemble folk? Did none of you pay heed to Capiam's warning? They're dying like flies at Ruatha!'

'Then why are you here, sir?' my rather stupid brother Campen had the gall to ask.

'What did you say?' Father drew himself up like a dragon about to flame, and even Campen drew back from the contained fury in his stance. How Campen escaped a clout I did not then understand.

'But – but – but Capiam said quarantine. . . .'

Father tilted his handsome head up, and extended his arms, palms up and outwards, to fend off a proximity none of us was at all likely to make.

'I am in quarantine from any of you as of this moment. I shall immure myself in my quarters, and none of you', he said, shaking his heavy forefinger at us, 'shall come near me until' – he paused dramatically – 'that period is over and I know myself to be clean.'

'Is the disease infectious? How contagious is it?' I heard

35

myself asking, because it was important for us to establish that.

'Either way I shall not jeopardize my family.' His expression was so noble I nearly laughed.

Nor did any of my siblings dare ask further about our mother and sisters.

'All messages are to be slipped under my door. Food will be left in the hall. That is all.'

With that, he motioned us aside and stomped into the Hold. We could follow his progress across the Hall and to the stairs by the angry pounding of his boots on the flagstones. Then a sort of muffled sob broke the spell.

'What of Mother?' Mostar asked, his eyes wide with anxiety.

'What of Mother indeed!' I said. 'Well, let's not stand here, making a spectacle of ourselves.' I cocked my head towards the roadway where small groups of cotholders had gathered, attracted first by the dragon's arrival and our tableau on the Hold steps.

Of one accord we retired into the Hall. I was not the only one to glance up at the now closed door to the first level.

'It isn't fair,' Campen began, sitting down heavily in the nearest chair. I knew that he meant Father's early return.

'She'd know how to cure us,' Gallen said, fear in his eyes.

'So do I, for she trained me,' I said curtly, for I think I knew then that Mother would not return. And it was also important for the family not to panic or give any show of apprehension. 'We're a hardy lot, Gallen. You know that. You've never been sick in your life.'

'I had the spotted fever.'

'We all had that,' Mostar said derisively, but the rest of them began to relax.

'He oughtn't to have broken quarantine, though,' Theskin said very thoughtfully. 'It doesn't set a good example. Alessan ought to have kept him at Ruatha.'

I wondered about that, too, although Father can be so overbearing that even Lords older than himself have given way to his wishes. I didn't like to think that Alessan was ineffective, even if he had courteously deferred to Father's wishes. A quarantine was a quarantine!

That night I fell easily into an exhausted sleep but, too restless to sleep well, I awoke very early again. It was so early, in fact, that none of the day staff was about his duties, and I picked up the note tucked under my father's door. I nearly tore it up when I'd read the message. Oh, the stock of febrifuges he wanted and the wine and food staples were understandable, but he instructed Campen to bring Anella, and 'her family' as he put it, into the safety of the Hold. So he would leave my mother and sisters in danger at Ruatha yet ask his oldest son and heir to bring his mistress to safety? And the two children he had sired on her.

Oh, it was no scandal really. Mother had always ignored the matter. She'd had practice over the Turns, and indeed once I had overheard her say to one of the aunts that relief now and then from his attentions was welcomed. But I didn't like Anella. She simpered, she clung and, if Father couldn't pretend interest in her, she was quite as happy on Mostar's arm. Indeed, I think she hoped to be wed to my brother. I longed to tell her that Mostar had other ideas. Still, I wondered if her last son was my father's issue or Mostar's.

I chided myself for such snide thoughts. At least the child had a strong family resemblance. With my belt knife, I separated the slip of hide into its two messages and slid Campen's portion under his door. I bore the discreet half down to the kitchen where sleepy drudges were folding up their pallets before starting their chores. My presence provoked tentative smiles and some apprehension, so I smiled reassurances and told the brightest of the lot what to put on Lord Tolocamp's morning tray.

Campen met me in the Hall, distractedly waving his portion of our father's orders. 'What am I to do about this, Rill? I can hardly ride out of the Hold proper and bring her back in broad daylight.'

'Bring her in from the fire-heights. No one'll be looking there today.'

'I don't like it, Rill. I just don't like it.'

'When have our likes or dislikes ever mattered, Campen?'

Anxious to get out of range of his querulous confusion, I went off to inspect the Nurseries on the southern side of the storey. Here, at least, was an island of serenity – well, as serene as twenty-nine babes and toddlers can be. The girls were going about their routine tasks under the watchful gaze of Aunt Lucil and her assistants. With all the babble there, they would not have heard the drums clearly enough to be worried yet. Since the Nursery had its own small kitchen, I would have to remember to have them close off their section if Fort Hold did surrender to the disease. And I must also remember to have additional supplies sent up – just to be on the safe side.

I checked on the laundry and linen stores, and suggested to the Wash Aunt that today, being sunny and not too chill, was an excellent day to do a major wash. She was a good person, but tended to procrastinate out of a mistaken notion that her drudges were woefully overworked. I knew Mother always had to give her a push to get started. I didn't like to think that I was usurping any of my mother's duties, even on a temporary basis, but we might be in need of every length of clean linen ever woven in the Hold.

The weavers, when I arrived in the Loft cots, were diligently applying themselves to their shuttles. One great roll of the sturdy mixed yarns, on which my mother prided herself, was just being clipped free of the woof. Aunt Sira greeted me with her usual cool, contained manner. Although she must have heard some of the drum messages over the clack of heddle and shuttle, she made no comment on the world outside.

I had a late breakfast in the little room on the first

sub-level, which Mother called her 'office', as grateful as she must often have been for this retreat. Still the drums rolled, acknowledging and then passing on the dire tidings. One didn't hear it only once, sad to say, but several times. I winced the fourth time Keroon's code came through, and hummed loudly to keep the latest message from adding to the misery already in my heart. Ruatha was close by. Why had we no messages from them, no reassurance from my mother and my sisters?

A knock on the door interrupted these anxieties, and I was almost glad to learn that Campen awaited me on the first storey. Halfway up the stairs, I realized that he must have returned with Anella and that, if he was on the first storey, she was expecting to have guest quarters. I myself would have put her on the inner corridor of the fifth storey. But the apartment at the end of the first storey was more than appropriate for her. There was no way that I would accommodate her in my mother's suite, with its convenient access to Father's sleeping-room. My father was, after all, in isolation, and my mother was alive in Ruatha.

Anella had obeyed Tolocamp's instruction to the letter. She had brought not only her two babies but also her mother, father, three younger brothers, and six of the frailer of her family dependants. How they managed to climb the fire-heights I did not enquire, but two of them looked about to collapse. They could go to the upper storeys and be attended by our own elderlies. Anella pouted a bit at being assigned rooms so far from Tolocamp, but neither Campen nor I paid any attention to her remarks or to those of her shrewish mother. I was just relieved that the entire hold had not descended on us. I suspected the older two brothers had more sense than to chance their arms on their pert sister's prospects. Although I felt Anella ought to be well able to care for her children, I did assign her two servants, one from the Nursery level and a general. I wished to have no complaints from my father about her reception or quar-

39

ters. Any guest would have had as much courtesy from me. But I didn't have to like it.

Then I sped down to the kitchens to discuss the day with Felim. He needed only to be told he was doing splendidly. The kitchens are always the worst places for rumour and gossip. Fortunately, no one there understood the coded messages, although they must have recognized that the drum tower was unusually busy. Sometimes one knows the drums are relaying good news, happy tidings. The beat seems brighter, higher-pitched, as if the very skins are singing with pleasure at their work. So, if I fancied that the drums were weeping today, who could blame me?

Towards evening, mistakes were made in the messages relayed as weary drummer arms faltered in the beat. I was forced to endure repetitions – despairing pleas from Keroon and Telgar for healers to replace those who had died of the disease they tried to cure. I put plugs in my ears so that I could sleep. Even so, my eardrums seemed to echo the pulse of the day's grievous news.

Chapter Four

3.14.43

ONE OF THE PLUGS FELL OUT during my restless sleep, so I heard the drums all too clearly that morning when they beat out the news of my mother's death, and then the deaths of my sisters. I dressed and went to comfort Lilla, Nia and Mara. Gabin crept in, his face reddened with the effort not to cry in public. He howled as he buried his head in my shoulder. And I cried, too. For my sisters and for myself who had not wished them a safe and happy journey.

My brothers, all but Campen, sought us out during the morning and so we had the luxury of private grief. I wonder if any of us hoped that Tolocamp would fall ill of the disease he had left our mother and sisters to die from.

When a messenger from Desdra found me, I welcomed him as an excuse to leave the sorrow-filled room. I could have gone down the back stairs to the stores to fill Desdra's request for supplies, but I led the man through the main corridor. Clearly I heard my father's vigorous voice calling out of the window, and I saw Anella lurking just round the first bend in the corridor. Quick as a snake, she scuttled away, but the gloating smirk on her face provoked me past indifference to active dislike and disgust of her.

41

The healer apprentice was hard-pressed to keep up with me as I whipped down the spiral stairs to the lower levels. When I piled sack upon sack of the herbs and root medicines that Desdra had listed, he protested that he wouldn't be able to lug so much to the Healer Hall. I summoned a drudge, my voice almost a shriek, and the scared Sim rushed in answer, his eyes round with fear that he had somehow forgotten something important.

Controlling myself, I apologized to the healer for over-burdening him. I would have merely ordered a second drudge to assist Sim and the healer, but as I entered the kitchen passage I caught sight of Anella sweeping down the steps, beckoning imperiously to Felim. I knew that if I entered the main kitchen and saw that smug little lay-aback playing Lady Holder I would rue the outcome. Instead, I left by the side-door with healer and drudge. The chill afternoon air enveloped and cooled me, though I set a brisk pace for my companions.

The Harper Hall was in an uproar when I got there, alive with shouts and cries of joy. I couldn't imagine what occasioned such joy, but it was contagious and I smiled without knowing why, just relieved to hear some happiness. Then the voices became separated and an unmistakable baritone rang clearly.

'Fog caught me between holds, friends,' Master Tirone was saying in clarion tones. 'And a lame runner. I caught a fresh mount from a pasture and was proceeding on when I heard the first drum message. I came on apace, I can tell you, and never stopped for sleep or food. I'll apologize for borrowing the runners later, when the drums are not so hot with important messages.' The sly hint of laughter in his voice was rewarded by chuckles from the other harpers. 'It was shorter to take the back route by then, so how was I to know Lord Tolocamp had set up guards to prevent any of us entering or leaving?' That was the first I'd heard of my father's precautions. Master Tirone's voice dropped to a more confidential tone. 'Now, what's this about an internment camp for healer or harper trying to contact his Hall? How are we supposed to work with such a foolish restriction on movement?'

The healer eyed me with some consternation, for this smacked of criticism of the Lord Holder. I could not in conscience show any trace of my growing disgust, disillusionment and distrust of my sire. And obviously I should not have overheard such sentiment.

Then Desdra herself appeared from the far side of the Hall court, her face lighting with relief as she saw how burdened we were. 'Lady Nerilka, I only asked for interim supplies.'

'I recommend that you take as much as you can get before I am no longer in a position to help.'

She did not question me, but I saw her eyes accept my words and the implications of my tone.

'I renew my offer to nurse the sick, wherever and whoever they might be,' I said as firmly as I could as she took the sacks from my arms.

'You must take your mother's place here during this emergency, Lady Nerilka,' she said, her voice low and kind, her deep-set and expressive eyes conveying her sympathy and condolences. I had once thought the journeywoman too passive a practitioner, her manner too detached, but I had misjudged her. How could I tell her, now, that she mistook my measure and circumstances? Or had such a trivial matter as Anella's arrival not percolated through to the two Halls?

'How is Master Capiam?' I asked, before she could turn away.

'He has nearly completed the course of the disease.' Desdra's voice rippled with wry humour, and I detected a twinkle in her eyes. 'He's too cantankerous to die, and determined to find a cure for this plague. Thank you, Lady Nerilka.'

Our brief exchange had outlasted the audible conversations from the Harper Hall, so there was nothing for me to do but retrace my steps out of the court, with Sim trotting behind me. Poor Sim. I forget he has short legs and cannot match my long stride.

'Sim, where is this internment camp of Lord Tolocamp's?' I sought any excuse to avoid returning to the Hold for a little while. My anger was too sharp, my grief too fresh, my self-discipline nonexistent.

Sim pointed to his right, where the great road south dips down into a small valley through a copse of trees. I walked far enough down the broad roadway to have an uninterrupted view, and saw guards pacing the arbitrary boundaries.

'Are there many wayfarers halted there?'

Sim nodded, his eyes frightened. 'Harper and healer, all only trying to get back to their Halls. And a few of the holdless. We always have them coming along. But there'll be sick ones, soon. Wanting help from the Healer Hall. What'll they do? They got a right to healing.'

So they had. Even my mother was – had been – generous to the holdless.

'Do the guards allow anyone into the valley?'

Sim nodded. 'But not back out again.'

'Who's the guard leader?'

'Theng, far as I know.'

Even Theng could be got round if it was done the right way. He enjoyed a bottle of wine, and while he was drinking he could pretend not to see past the end of the flask. Harper and healer refused access to their Halls? My father was foolish as well as frightened. And hypocritical when he, himself, returning from a disease-ridden Hold, placed his own people in jeopardy by his very presence. Well, that didn't mean that I had to be foolish, too. I knew my duty to the Halls – hadn't my father drilled it into me? And I might need their charity before the end of these terrible days. I would speak to Felim, and to Theng.

As I walked back up to the Hold, I saw a figure in a first-storey window. My father? Yes, that was his window, and he was watching Sim and me. Sim he wouldn't distinguish from any other drudge wearing Hold livery, but just how keen was his long sight? And what would it matter if he identified me? It would probably be the first time he had. I strode on, proud and careless. But I did take the side-entrance into the kitchens. I had to speak to Felim, didn't I?

'What am I to do now, Lady Nerilka?' the cook began before I could ask him to save the broken meats for the interned men. 'She came down with orders for all kinds of food that I know Lady Pendra would not condone—' And then he burst into tears again, blotting his eyes and face with the rag he always had hanging out of his apron waist. 'She was stern, Lady Pendra, but she was fair. A man knew he had only to keep to her standards and there'd be no complaint.'

'What did Anella want?'

'She said she was to order Hold matters now. And I was to prepare broth for her children, whose stomachs are delicate; and there are to be confections with every meal, for her parents desire sweets; and roasts midday and evening. Lady Nerilka, you know that isn't possible.' Tears streamed down his cheeks again as he shrugged. 'Must I take orders from her now?'

'I'll find out, Felim. Proceed with the plans we made this morning. Not even for Anella can we alter an established routine in one day.'

Then I asked him to save what he could from the evening meal, for delivery to Theng.

'I took the liberty of sending the broken meats last night, Lady Nerilka. As your lady mother would have done. Oh, oh, she was fair, she was fair. . . .' He buried his face once more in his napkin.

Felim was fair, too, I thought, trying to keep my mind off my mother. Thinking of Anella helped. That little lay-aback, coming in here and thinking she could just take over a Hold the size of Fort and run it as if it were exactly like the backhills midden from which she'd come! The thought of the chaos that would shortly result at such inexpert hands gave me a perverse delight. Little did

Anella know of real management, and if she wished to keep my father content she'd better learn. Whatever had made her think that just because Lady Pendra was dead she was to step into her shoes, just as she had taken her bed partner? Unless. . . .

Once again I encountered a distressed Campen in the front hall. My brother's face was suffused with blood and his features contorted with dismay. Doral, Mostar and Theskin, who were deep in low conversation with him, wore the same expression.

'Isn't there anything we can *do*?' Theskin was demanding, his fingers clenching and unclenching on the hilt of his belt knife.

Doral was slamming one fist into the other palm. 'Nerilka, where have you been? Do you know what has happened?'

'Anella's moving in.'

'Father has had her transferred into Mother's rooms. Already!' There was no doubt of the outrage that Campen and the others felt. 'He's looking for you, Rill, demanding to know where you've been all day, what you were doing at the internment camp – and whatever possessed you to go there?'

'To find out if it existed at all,' I replied, bitterly ignoring the other questions. 'When?'

'That was our early-morning task,' Theskin replied, indicating that Doral had assisted. 'Setting the guard and drawing up the watch rosters. Now this! Could he not wait a decent interval?'

'He may come down with the illness and have lost a last chance to enjoy his few remaining hours!'

'*Nerilka!*' Campen was appalled at my irreverence, but Theskin and Doral guffawed.

'She may have the answer, you know, Campie lad,' Theskin said. 'Our sire has ever liked his little pleasures.'

'Theskin, that is enough!' Campen remembered to lower his voice, but the intensity of his reprimand made up for the lack of volume.

Theskin shrugged. 'I'm off. Checking the guard! I'll be back for my dinner. Wouldn't miss that for the world!' He winked at me, tugged Doral by the arm, and they went off, leaving me with Campen.

But I had no wish for a continued lecture on my shortcomings. 'Watch out, Campen. She has two sons, you know, and we could all be booted to the upper storeys!'

Patently this had not occurred to my eldest brother. As he struggled with the possibility, I made it safely to my snug little inside room.

That evening's meal was one I do not remember eating, certainly not enjoying. Our dead mother had made courtesy in us such an instinctive reaction that we could not, any of us, be impolite despite that night's provocation. I had delayed my descent to the Main Hall, so I was rather surprised to find so many of our relations from the second storey. The great tables were set up; even my father's chair sat in place on the dais. Anella had been busy.

'Were you invited?' I asked Uncle Munchaun when he sauntered over to me.

'No, but she'd not know our ways, would she?'

One could count on Uncle Munchaun, not to mention the others, to sense a situation and make sure to witness it first hand.

'I fear I've found nothing of value in my reading thus far,' Uncle continued smoothly. 'I've set others to the task as well. Any word from the Halls? I understand you were there today.'

I ignored the thrust. 'Master Tirone has returned from that mediation. By the mountain trail.'

'Then he missed the additions to our Hold?'

'He may have. Certainly he missed the guards.'

'I almost wish he hadn't,' Uncle murmured, a gleam in his eyes. Then he touched my arm warningly and I turned to see Anella, followed by her parents, sweeping into the Great Hall.

Her grand entrance was spoiled by her flaming cheeks

47

and her father's stumbling pace. The man had not been drunk, I was later informed, but had a crippled foot. But I was in no mood to be charitable or compassionate. He, at least, had the grace to look embarrassed throughout the next few minutes.

Anella, dressed in a heavily embroidered gown totally unsuitable for the mourning of the Hold or for a family dinner, mounted the three steps to the dais and walked firmly to my mother's chair. Uncle Munchaun's hand restrained me now.

'Lord Tolocamp wishes me to read this message to you.' Her voice was strident in her effort to be heard and to project her new authority. She unrolled the message and held it up in front of her eyes, which bulged unbecomingly as she shouted at us.

'I, Lord Tolocamp, quarantined from active participation in the conduct of Fort Hold in these unsettled days, appoint and deputize Lady Anella as Lady Holder to ensure the management of the Hold until such time as our desired union can be publicly celebrated. My son, Campen, will actively discharge under my direction any duties required of the Lord Holder until such time as I am no longer immured.

'I solemnly charge all of you, under pain of disgrace and exile, to observe the quarantine of this Hold, and to refrain from contact with any others until such time as Master Capiam, or his delegate Masterhealer, rescinds the quarantine restrictions. I require obedience to all restrictions made by me to ensure the safety and health of Fort, Pern's first and largest Hold. Obey and we prosper. Deny and we fall.'

She turned the sheet towards us and pointed to the end. 'His signature and ring mark are here to be verified.' Then she insulted us again. 'He charges me to discover which of you ventured perilously close to the internment camp today.' Her bulging eyes swept the lot of us.

Just as I stepped forward, so did Peth, Jess, Nia and Gabin.

'Do not anger me,' Anella cried. 'Lord Tolocamp only told me about one of you.'

'We all must have had a look at one time or another,' said Jess, speaking out before I could gather my wits. 'I've never seen an internment camp.'

'Do you not understand? There are sick people there!' Anella's face turned pale with fright. 'If you catch the plague, you will infect the rest of us before you die.'

'Just like our Lord Holder,' came a voice from somewhere in her audience.

'Who said that? Who spoke so vilely?'

There was no answer, only a shifting of boots on the flagstones. Even I could not identify the speaker – to congratulate him, or her. My private wager would fall on Theskin.

'I will know who spoke!' Anella ranted on a bit more, but she would never learn the answer, having shattered any chance she might have had of gaining the trust and confidence of those in the Hall that night. 'Lord Tolocamp will hear of the snake at his bosom!'

She glared about the Hall one last time, then yanked at the heavily carved chair that my mother had filled so adequately. She was not strong enough to shift it, and a twitter greeted her attempt. Her mother signalled peremptorily to a drudge to assist her daughter. When Anella finally seated herself, her mother sat down beside her, the husband on her left. Those of us who ought to have taken our places on the dais declined to do so and, with a bit of angling, all were accommodated at the trestle tables.

'Where are Lord Tolocamp's children?' she demanded when we were arranged. 'Campen!' She pointed at him, for him she knew by sight. 'Theskin, Doral, Gallen. Assume your places.' She paused briefly; I could see her eyes blinking and an irritated twitch to her mouth. 'Nalka! Is she not the oldest living daughter?'

Uncle Munchaun nudged me. 'You'd best go, Rill, even misnamed, for your father will know if you insult her so publicly.'

I knew he was right. As I rose, I saw Anella's mother murmur something to her.

'And there is a harper in this Hold, is there not? We honour the harper.'

Casmodian rose, bowed, and managed a smile.

'Why did you seat yourselves below?' she demanded as Campen and Theskin mounted the dais steps.

'With all due respect, Lady Anella,' Theskin said with a wry smile, 'we thought your family would require the seating here.'

Though courteously spoken, Theskin's words were none the less a gibe, and she was not too dense to know it, even if she had no adequate retort. No one mentioned that she had not named all of Tolocamp's surviving mature children, so Peth, Jess and Gabin made a merrier meal than we others did.

Bravely, Casmodian sat next to the father. I think they were the only two to converse that evening at the head table. I know I tasted nothing of even the little food I forced myself to eat. Unfortunately, now I had time to think of all I had *not* done for my mother, of my uncharitable absence from the last moments my sisters had had at Fort Hold. I seethed, too, with fury at the usurper and vowed that I would not lift a hand to assist her in her new role. How convenient that she couldn't even remember my name properly. If I judged the temper of the Hall correctly, she would have no help from anyone, even in such a small matter as the correct nomenclature of Lord Tolocamp's children.

I drank more wine that evening than is my custom – or perhaps it was because I also ate so little. It was enough to finish the meal and slip from the Hall to the kitchens, to be sure that this new Lady Holder had not countermanded my order about the broken meats. Then, by the back stairs, I sought my own room and the solace of sleep.

Chapter Five

3.15.43

THE DRUMS WOKE ME AT DAWN, for in my giddiness I had forgotten to plug my ears. Then the message woke me completely – twelve Wings had flown Thread at Igen and all was well.

How could twelve Wings have flown out of Igen Weyr when half the dragonriders werc ill of the plague and the Weyr had already suffered deaths? They could not have mounted more than nine Wings if their casualties had been accurately reported, and there would be no advantage to prevaricate at this terrible moment.

I rose and dressed, then descended to the kitchens to surprise the drudges brewing the first of the many urns of klah. Its aromatic smell was a restorative all by itself, and the first fragrant cup was the best one of any day, heartening me all the more in my grief and dismay. I was stirring the porridge when Felim appeared, his face first brightening, then falling into a suitably lugubrious expression as he advanced on me.

'I was obliged to send basketfuls of untouched food to the camps, Lady Nerilka. Wasn't the dinner well enough?'

'Few of us had the heart to eat, Felim. It is no insult to you.'

51

'*She* complained that I did not offer sufficient choice of sweets,' he told me, offended. 'Has she any idea of the handicaps under which I labour? I cannot chop and change midday. There isn't a single apprentice or journeyman able to provide a choice of sweets on an hour's notice in such quantities as are needed in the Hall these days.'

I murmured phrases to soothe his damaged self-esteem, more out of habit than from a desire to redeem Anella in his eyes. A disgruntled cook could cause real problems in a Hold the size of Fort. Let Anella learn by her mistakes, and discover just how much hard work it was to be Lady Holder.

It was then that I realized the truth of her announcement: She was Lady Holder, and due all the courtesies and honours that had been my mother's. Well, there were certain private possessions of my mother's that would not fall into her hands. I said a few pacifying words to Felim, to ensure a decently cooked meal this evening, and rushed to my mother's office on the sub-level.

There I quickly removed all her private journals, her notes about this personality and that worker – we girls had long known her to jog her memory by these entries, and had done our best not to figure in them very often. They would be invaluable reading to Anella and hideously embarrassing to us, to have not only our childhood peccadilloes revealed, but also the problems of the second-storey occupants. Mother had some gems and jewellery that were hers in her own right, not Hold adornments which should by rights be divided among the surviving daughters. I doubted Anella's probity in distributing them, so I chose to undertake that task as well.

If Anella thought these things had been removed, she might search for them, so I hurried along the back passages to the stores and hid the two sacks of journals and the small parcel of jewellery on the top of a dusty shelf. Anella was hands shorter than I.

I was on my way back when Sim intercepted me.

'Lady Nerilka, *she* is asking for a Lady Nalka.'

'Is she? Well, there isn't one in the Hold, is there?'

Sim blinked, confused. 'Doesn't she mean you, lady?'

'She may indeed, but until she learns to call me by my proper name I am in no way obliged to answer, am I, Sim?'

'Not if you say so, Lady Nerilka.'

'So return to her, Sim, and say you cannot find Lady Nalka in the Hold.'

'Is that what I do?'

'That is what you do.'

He lumbered off, muttering under his breath about not finding Lady Nalka – any Lady Nalka – in the Hold. That is what he was to say. No Lady Nalka in the Hold.

I crossed the yard to the Harper Hall. Anella might have many things on her mind more important than the pharmaceutical stores, but eventually someone would inform her that it was Lady Nerilka whom she required. And she surely would tell my father of my insolence. When he emerged from his isolation, I had no doubt that he would deliver a thorough and painful chastisement. I might as well merit every blow. Meanwhile, it was my right to dispense those medicinal supplies as required, and I was determined that the healers would have full benefit of them.

I was directed to the Hall kitchens by a cheerful young apprentice and made my way there, reflecting that I seemed to be spending a lot more time in kitchens these days.

'I'll need the glass bottles sterilized, and that means fifteen minutes in water at the rolling boil and no cheating on the sands,' Desdra was saying to the journeyman. 'Now, I'll— Lady Nerilka!' There was about Desdra a buoyancy that had been absent the previous day.

'Master Capiam is better?'

'Himself again, I'm glad to say. Not everyone who gets the plague needs to die of it. Anyone ill in Fort Hold?'

'If you mean my sire, he keeps to his apartments but is well enough to issue orders.'

'So I heard.' Desdra's wry smile informed me that she found the change tasteless.

'While I am still in charge of the pharmacy, what are your needs?'

Desdra had turned to watch the journeyman, her mind clearly on more urgent matters. She looked back at me with a smile, however. 'Can you decoct, infuse and blend?'

'I supply all our medicinal needs.'

'Then, prepare a cough syrup – tussilago by preference. Here, let me give you the recipe that I have found efficacious." She had a scrap of hide in her hand, a charcoal stick in the other; hastily, but legibly, she scrawled measurements and ingredients. 'Don't balk at adding numbweed – that is the only thing that depresses the terrible racking cough.' Then she consulted another list in her hand. She was distracted by my presence. 'And has your mother—? Oh, I beg your pardon.' She touched my hand in apology, her eyes troubled to have caused me pain. 'Have you a restorative soup? We shall need kettles of restorative soups.'

I thought of Felim's reaction to yet another bizarre request, but the small night-hearth could be used, and all kinds of scraps go into the soup-pot. The last place Anella would think to find me would be in the hot, small inner kitchen.

'Cook, cool it into jelly. It'll transport better that way.' She had one eye on the sands that were only grains away from her fifteen-minutes-at-the-rolling-boil.

I left her to her task, hoping it bode well. There was a suppressed excitement about Desdra that could not be due entirely to the Master Harper's recovery. Was she brewing a cure?

Fortunately it took all day to concoct both the restorative soup and Desdra's cough syrup. The tussilago really did numb the lining of the throat. I improved the taste

54

with a harmless flavouring and filled two demijohns with the mixture, reserving a large flask for Hold use, should it be required. I made a note of the syrup in the Record.

When Sim and I brought the products of my day's labours over to the Hall, the air of suppressed excitement that I had noted in Desdra was now rampant, but I could find out nothing from the journeyman who took syrup and soup from me. He thanked me profusely enough, but plainly had other tasks pending.

It was hard to wish to help, to be capable of offering capable help, and not find a market for it, I thought as I plodded back across the night-dark yard. There were lights on in my father's quarters and in what had been my mother's. But no one was at the window, spying on unidentifiable flaunters of stupid rules.

I looked over my shoulder at the despicable internment camp and saw the guards on their rounds between the glowbasket standards. Was that where my soup and syrup would go? If that was its destination, my day had been profitable. With my spirits lifted, I continued back to the Hold.

Chapter Six

3.16.43

CAMPEN FOUND ME the next morning preparing to make more soup. 'So this is where you are! Anella is looking for you.'

'She's been looking for a Lady Nalka, and there is no one by that name in the Hold.'

Campen snorted with disgust. 'You know perfectly well she means you.'

'Then she should summon me by name. I'll not go otherwise.'

'In the meantime, she's making life very difficult for our sisters, and they miss our mother enough without having to put up with her carpings.'

I was instantly repentant. In my own misery and guilt, I had forgotten that Lilla and Nia needed my presence and support.

'She must have new gowns, suitable to her position. Your needlework is the best.'

'Kista was the best needlewoman among us,' I told him angrily. 'And Merin sewed the straightest seam. But I'll go.'

It was not a pleasant interview, and I knew that my behaviour could be faulted on several counts. To add insult to injury, Anella was younger than I by several

Turns, and keenly aware of that and of my greater height. But, knowing that I had deliberately disregarded her summonses, I took the tongue-lashing in silence, and took some consolation in the fact that she had to crane her neck at an awkward angle to berate me. She looked like a wherry hen, strutting about in a heavy dressing-gown far too ornate to suit her thin body and falling off her bottle-necked shoulders so that she had to jerk it frequently back into place. She lacked dignity, experience, sense and humour.

'So how do you account for your absence these past two days? Where have you been? For if· you've been sneaking off to meet some holder—'

At that accusation I decided I had had enough of her rantings. 'I have been preparing restorative soups and cough syrups, and checking our medicinal supplies in case they should be needed.' She flushed at my reminder of the present crisis. 'The pharmacy has been my responsibility in this Hold.'

'Why wasn't I told that was where you were? Your father—' She abruptly closed her lips.

'My father would not have known my especial duties. It was my mother's place to order such domestic affairs.'

She gave me a searching glance, but I had kept my voice bland and chosen my words carefully.

'No one around here tells me anything I need to know,' she complained. 'If your name is not Nalka, what is it?'

'Nerilka.'

'Close enough. Why did you not come at my bidding?' She grew angry again.

'I was not told.'

'But they knew you were the one I wanted to see!'

'The entire Hold is still distracted by grief and anxiety.'

She clamped her lips into a thin line, but what she wished to say was sparking out of her eyes, which were beginning once again to protrude with her attempts to control her agitations. She swished off to the window and stood looking out, twitching the gown back up her shoulders several times. Abruptly she whirled back.

'Your mother had everything so well organized in this Hold that I'm sure she had drapery stores and patterns. You may come with me to choose suitable lengths for my new wardrobe.'

'Aunt Sira is in charge of Weaving.'

'I don't need the Weaving Aunt. I need your sewing skills. You have those as well, do you not?' When I nodded, she went on: 'Now, where are the keys?' I pointed to the small chest on top of the press. With a cry of exasperation she leaped towards it, wrenching the drawer out in her haste to secure the keys to her new dignities. She had to hold the massive ring in both hands. 'But which one? And which unlocks the jewellery-safe? And the spice-cupboard?'

'The storeys are colour-coded. The housekeeping keys are the smaller ones, room keys the larger. Hall keys larger still, and gold. All kitchen stores are green.'

So I was forced to spend the rest of the morning taking my stepmother from storey to storey and as far down the sub-levels as she insisted we go. I answered every question willingly and fully, but volunteered no information without seeming to withhold any. Afterwards, I don't know if I was more disgusted with myself or with her general ignorance of Hold management. Had her mother not required her to do anything, and she the only daughter in the hold? I only hoped that my father would rue the day he let his infatuation overwhelm common sense. And the inconsistency of his complaint against my one suitor, Garben, who came from, no more or less, the same sort of family as Anella's. I also knew suddenly, and with complete certainty, that I would not be in Fort Hold to see his awakening to reality.

Anella required my presence to cut and start seaming several gowns for herself. She had some sense in her, for she said that Lilla and Nia could have tunics from the remnants of the three lengths. That ensured their co-operation and diligence on her clothes. I excused myself

58

as soon as the work was well started, on the pretext that I must discharge my duties as pharmacist.

And so, in the Harper Hall, I learned for the first time of the blood serum injections that had been administered just the day before, and I heard, in a somewhat garbled fashion, of Master Capiam's recollection of this ancient method of giving a small dose of a disease to prevent a more disastrous illness. Healers had been given the first injections, as they would most need protection against the plague. Master Fortine had succumbed to it, received the treatment, and was suffering only minor discomfort. Soon, very soon, there would be enough of this liquid miracle to prevent any more healthy people from suffering the rigours of the plague. Pern was saved!

I took leave to doubt that enthusiastic report, but certainly the whole atmosphere of the Hall was charged with hope and relief. I immediately returned to the Hold, reprieved from the despair of more deaths among my loved ones. I rushed up to the sewing-room to tell my sisters the good news. Anella was there, of course, supervising their stitches. She questioned me closely, making me repeat my news several times before she rushed off. Maybe she actually cared more for my father's health than for his Hold.

How it came to be, I do not know, but by evening three healers arrived at the Hold and were shown immediately up to my father's quarters. I assume they inoculated him first. I'm certain that Anella was second, and then her babes. To my complete surprise, the immediate family was also injected, my younger sisters enduring the prick of the needlethorn without a whimper.

'There's enough left for fifteen more, Lady Nerilka. Whom would you suggest?' the healer journeyman asked me. 'Desdra said you'd know.' He had spoken quietly to me as I received the injection.

I told him to do all the Nursery adults, our three harpers, Felim and his chief assistant, Uncle Munchaun, and Sira, for she alone knew all the brocade patterns that

59

were our especial Hold pride. And the chief bailiff, Barndy, and his son. With my father still immured in his rooms, Barndy was a key person and his son only slightly less so. Munchaun would take their part if that became necessary, and he was the only one who would shout Tolocamp down without reprisal.

3.17.43

I was required to spend most of the morning sewing in Anella's presence while she stood over my sisters and me, criticizing our stitches, making us pick out and do over – as often as not missing our poorer work – until I could stand it no more. Lilla, Nia and Mara were more inclined to diligence, since they could anticipate, I hoped, to have new tunics for their labours.

Anella also had the poor taste to recount to us Tolocamp's injunctions to his bailiff and my brothers that there was to be no disposition of Fort Hold's stores to the indigent. All must be reserved for the needs of Fort Hold's dependants. This was a critical time, and Fort must stand firm, as an example to the rest of the continent. For instance, Anella relished reporting, Tolocamp was certain that the Healer and Harper would be applying to the Hold for substantial aid of food and medicine. He had received a formal request for an interview with Master Capiam and Master Tirone the next morning.

That, for me, was the final straw. I had now come to the end of patience, courtesy and filial loyalty. I could no longer endure that woman's presence or remain a dependant of a man whose cowardice and parsimony made a disgrace of my Bloodline. I would no longer remain in a dishonoured Hold.

On the grounds that I had a confectionery recipe that I wished to prepare for the evening meal, I excused myself. I went down to the kitchens, and on to the dispensary. There I distilled fellis in the largest kettle and brewed an equally large batch of the tussilago syrup. While these were simmering, I rifled the overstuffed shelves, taking a generous portion of every herb, root, stalk, leaf, blossom and tuber that might possibly be of use to the Healer Hall. These I packaged, tying them securely and leaving them in a shadowy corner of the inner storeroom against the unlikely chance that Anella might inspect the facility. I decanted the fellis and tussilago into padded demijohns and added to these surreptitious stores a pack containing clothing necessities for myself. Then I made the sticky sweet for the evening meal, enough to surfeit Anella and her parents.

That evening I sought out Uncle Munchaun and gave him my mother's jewels to distribute to my sisters.

'Like that, eh?' He hefted the hide-wrapped packet of jewellery. 'Did you not keep some by you?'

'A few pieces. I doubt jewellery will be required where I intend to go from here.'

'Send me word when you can, Rill. I shall miss you.'

'And I you, Uncle. You'll keep watch over my sisters?'

'Have I not always done so?'

'Better than most.' I could not say more or weaken my resolution, so I fled down the steps from the second storey.

3.18.43

The next day, I had dutifully started yet another kettle of restorative soup in the small kitchen when I saw the Masterharper and the Masterhealer making their way across the Great Court for their interview with Tolocamp. I caught Sim's attention and told him to take two others and wait for me outside the dispensary. I had a task to be done.

I changed from my dress into garb suitable for what I

61

hoped to be allowed to do, and stuffed a few last personal things in my belt pouch. I caught a glimpse of myself in the little mirror on my wall. It took me a moment: my hair had been my one vanity. I picked up the scissors and ruthlessly, before my resolution faltered, I cut off my long plaits and stuffed them into the darkest corner of the press. No one would think to search my room for some time to come. My shorn hair suited my new role in life.

With a leather thong, I tied back what was left of my thick black hair. Then I left the room that had been my refuge since my eighteenth summer and made my way down the spiral stairs to my father's first-storey apartment.

There was a convenient alcove on the inner wall just beyond the main door to his quarters. I had no sooner taken up my position when the drums announced the happy tidings that Orlith had laid a fine clutch of twenty-five eggs, including a queen egg. I'll bet there was considerable jubilation at Fort Weyr on that score. And it was certainly heartening news, though suddenly I could hear my father's mournful tones. Was he displeased with twenty-five and a queen? In ordinary times he would have called for wine to celebrate.

There was no one in the Hall, and at this hour in the morning most would be about their duties in or outside the Hold. I stepped close to the door and, by putting my ear to the wood, was able to hear most of what was said. Both Capiam and Tirone had good strong voices, and as they became more annoyed their voices rose. It was my father who mumbled.

'Twenty-five with a queen egg is a superb clutch this late in a Pass,' Capiam was saying.

'Moreta . . . mumble . . . Kadith . . . Sh'gall . . . so ill.'

'That is not *our* business,' I heard Master Tirone remark. 'Not that the illness of the rider has any effect on the performance of the dragon. Anyway, Sh'gall is flying Fall at Nerat, so he's evidently fully recovered.'

I had known that both Fort Weyrleaders had been ill and had recovered, for Jallora had been hastily dispatched from the Healer Hall when the Weyr healer had died. Why Sh'gall was flying at Nerat was beyond my source of information.

'I wish they would inform us of the status of each Weyr,' my father said. 'I worry so.'

'The *Weyrs*' – Tirone spoke with emphasis – 'have been discharging their traditional duties to their Holds!'

'Did *I* bring illness to the Weyrs?' my father demanded, more loudly and quite petulantly, I thought. 'Or the Holds? If the dragonriders were not too quick to fly here and there—'

'And Lords Holder not so eager to fill every nook and cranny of their—' Capiam was angry, too.

'This is *not* the time for recriminations!' Tirone interrupted them quickly. 'You know as well as, if not better than, most people, Tolocamp, that seamen introduced that abomination on to the continent!' The Masterharper's voice dripped with disapproval. I hoped my father was fully aware of it. 'Let us resume the discussion interrupted by such good news. I have men seriously ill in that camp of yours. There is not enough vaccine to mitigate the disease, but they could at least have the benefit of decent quarters and practical nursing.'

So I had been correct in my assumption that my father's parsimonious attitude extended to the two Halls that Fort had traditionally supplied generously whenever approached.

'Healers are among them,' my father countered in a sullen tone. 'Or so you tell me!'

'Healers are not immune to the viral influence and they cannot work without medicines,' Capiam said urgently. 'You have a great storehouse of medicinal supplies—'

'Garnered and prepared by my lost Lady—' How dare he speak in that maudlin fashion of my mother!

'Lord Tolocamp' – and I could hear the irritation in Master Capiam's voice – 'we *need* those supplies—'

'For Ruatha, eh?'

Surely my father didn't blame Ruatha for the tragedy?

'Other holds besides Ruatha have needs!' Capiam replied, as if Ruatha was indeed the very last one on his list.

'Supplies are the responsibility of the individual holder. Not mine. I cannot further deplete resources that might be needed by my own people.'

'If the Weyrs' – and Tirone's deep voice rang with feeling as he took up the argument – 'stricken as they are, can extend *their* responsibilities in the magnificent way they have, beyond the areas beholden to them, then how can you refuse?'

I was stuhned at my father's insensitive reply. 'Very easily. By saying no. No one may pass the perimeter into the Hold from any outlying area. If they don't have the plague, they have other, equally infectious, diseases. I shall not risk more of my people. I shall make no further contributions from my stores.'

Had my father not heard a single one of the messages, announcing the thousands of deaths in Keroon, Ista, Igen, Telgar and Ruatha? My mother and four sisters were dead and quite likely the guards and the servants who had accompanied them, but they numbered only forty in all, not four hundred or four thousand or forty thousand.

'Then, I withdraw my healers from your Hold.' I nearly cheered Capiam's statement.

'But – you – you can't *do* that!'

'Indeed he can. *We* can,' Master Tirone replied. I heard the scrape of his chair as he pushed it back from the table. I clapped my hands over my mouth lest I make any sound. 'Craftsmen are under the jurisdiction of their Hall. You'd forgotten that, hadn't you?'

I had just enough time to get back into the shadows as the door was pulled roughly open and Capiam swung into the hall. The light from my father's windows showed me the anger on the Masterhealer's face. Master Tirone slammed the door shut.

'I call them out! Then I'll join you in the camp.'

'I didn't think it would come to this!' Capiam was grim.

I inhaled, afraid for one moment that they might renege – this opposition was just what Tolocamp needed to bring him back to his lost senses.

'Tolocamp has presumed once too often on the generosity of the Halls! I hope this example reminds others of our prerogatives.'

'Call our Craftspeople out, but don't come to the camp with me, Tirone. You must stay in the Hall with your people, and guide mine!'

'My people' – Tirone gave a harsh laugh – 'with very few exceptions, are languishing in that blighted camp of his. You are the one who must bide at the Hall.'

I knew then where I would go when I left this Hold, and I knew what I could do to expiate my father's intransigence.

'Master Capiam' – I stepped forward – 'I have the storeroom keys.' I held up the duplicates my mother had given me on my sixteenth birthday.

'How did you . . .?' Tirone began, leaning forward to peer at my face. He didn't know who I was any more than Capiam did, but they knew I was one of the Fort Horde.

'Lord Tolocamp made plain his position when he received the request for medicines. I helped harvest and preserve them.'

'Lady . . .?' Capiam waited for me to speak my name, but his voice was kind and his manner gentle.

'Nerilka,' I said quickly, for I didn't expect so exalted a man to have known it. 'I have the right to offer you the products of my own labour.' Tirone was realizing that I had eavesdropped on their conversation, but I hardly cared. 'There is just one condition.' I let the keys swing from my fingers.

'If it is within my giving,' Capiam replied tactfully.

'That I may leave this Hold in your company and work with the sick in that horrid camp. I've been vaccinated.

65

Lord Tolocamp was expansive that day. Be that as it may, I will not stay in a Hold to be abused by a girl younger than myself. Tolocamp permitted her and her family to enter this hallowed Hold from the fire-heights, yet he leaves healers and harpers to die out there!' I nearly added, 'as he left my mother and sisters to die at Ruatha.' Instead I pulled at Capiam's sleeve. 'This way, quickly.'

Tolocamp would recover from his shock at their ultimatum and start roaring for Barndy or one of my brothers.

'I'll remove our Craftspeople from this Hold on my way out,' Tirone said. He turned and walked the other way.

'Young woman, you do realize that once you leave the Hold without your father's knowledge, particularly in his present frame of mind—'

'Master Capiam, I doubt he'll notice I'm gone.' Maybe he was the one who had told Anella that my name was Nalka. 'These steps are very steep,' I warned, suddenly remembering that the Masterhealer wasn't used to the back ways. I flicked on a handglow.

Capiam stumbled once or twice as we spiralled down, and I heard him draw a sigh of relief as we turned into the larger corridor towards the storerooms. Sim was lounging on the bench with the other two.

'You are prompt, I see.' I nodded reassurance at Sim, who hadn't expected to see the Masterhealer down here. 'Father appreciates promptness.' I included Master Capiam in that remark as I opened the door.

I went in first, flicking open the glowbaskets, and heard Capiam exclaim now that he recognized the room where he and my mother had often treated the Hold sick. I went into the main storeroom.

'Behold, Master Capiam, the produce of my labours since I was old enough to snip leaf and blossom or dig root and bulb. I won't say I have filled every shelf, but my sisters who have pre-deceased me would not deny me their portions. Would that all of these hoarded supplies were usable, but even herbs and roots lose their potency in time. Waste, that's the bulk of what you see, fattening tunnel snakes.' I had heard the slither as the reptiles fled from the glowlights. 'Carry-yokes are in the corner there, Sim.' I raised my voice now, for my other remarks had been for the Masterhealer's ears so that he knew that what I gave him today did not seriously deplete those treasured stores Tolocamp must reserve for his own people. 'You and the others, take up the bales.' When I saw them start to load up, I turned to Master Capiam. 'Master Capiam, if you do not mind – that's the fellis juice. I'll take this.' I hefted the other demijohn by its girth strap and slung the pack over my shoulder. 'I mixed fresh tussilago last night, Master Capiam. That's right, Sim. On your way now. We'll use the kitchen exit. Lord Tolocamp has been complaining again about the wear on the main-hall carpets,' I said quite mendaciously. 'It's as well to comply with his instructions even if it does mean extra lengths for the rest of us.'

I covered the glowbaskets and set down the demijohn to lock the storeroom, ignoring Capiam's expression. It didn't matter what he thought as long as I could leave the Hold without being seen.

'I would like to take more, but four drudges added to the noon parade to the perimeter are not going to be noticed by the guard.' He spared a look at my clothing then. 'No one will care in the least if one of the drudges continues on to the camp. Nor will anyone at the kitchen exit think it odd for the Masterhealer to leave with supplies.' I had accustomed them to such traffic to the Hall. 'Indeed, they would wonder if you left empty-handed.'

I had finished locking up and now I dangled the keys before me. I couldn't just hang them on the door. 'One never knows, does one?' I commented, stuffing them back into my belt pouch. 'My stepmother has another set. She thinks it is the only one. But *my* mother thought the stillroom a very good occupation for me. This way, Master Capiam.'

He followed me, and I kept expecting any moment to hear an exhortation or good advice.

'Lady Nerilka, if you leave now –'

'I *am* leaving –'

'– and in this fashion, Lord Tolocamp—'

I stopped in my tracks and faced the man. It wouldn't do to be heard arguing with him as we crossed the kitchen. '– will miss neither me nor my dower.' As I hefted the demijohn, I saw Sim exiting by the side-door, and thought I had best be at his heels or he might falter. 'I can be of real use in the internment camp, for I know about mixing medicines and decocting and infusing herbs. I shall be doing something constructive that is needed rather than sitting comfortably in a corner somewhere.' I did not add sewing straight seams to adorn my stepmother. 'I know your craftsmen are overworked. Every hand is needed.

'Besides' – I touched the keys in my pouch – 'I can slip back in whenever it's necessary. Don't look surprised. The drudges do it all the time. Why shouldn't I?' Especially when I am dressed as a drudge, I noted wryly.

I had to catch up to Sim and the others to maintain our cover; I also had to remember to move like a drudge. As I passed under the lintel of the kitchen door, I slumped my shoulders, lowered my head, canted my knees at each other for a more awkward gait, and pretended to be weighed down by my burdens, scuffing my feet in the dust.

Master Capiam was looking to our left, to the main forecourt and stairs where Master Tirone was moving down the ramp along with the healers who tended our elderlies, and the three harpers.

'He'll be watching them! Not us,' I told Master Capiam, for I, too, had caught sight of my father's figure in the open window. Maybe he'd catch his death of a cold. 'Try to walk less proudly, Master Capiam. You are, for the moment, merely a drudge, burdened and reluctantly heading for the perimeter, terrified of coming down sick to die like everyone in the camp.'

'Everyone in the camp is not dying.'

'Of course not,' I said hastily, hearing the anger in his voice. 'But Lord Tolocamp thinks so. He has so informed us constantly. Ah, a belated attempt on his part to prevent the exodus!' I caught sight of the helmet tips over the balustrade. 'Don't pause!' The Masterhealer had stopped briefly, and I didn't want anything to call attention to us. The departure of healers and harpers was a useful diversion. 'You can walk as slowly as you want, that's in character, but don't stop.'

I kept my head turned to the left but, then, drudges were always attempting to ignore what they were supposed to be doing in favour of any activity that appeared more interesting. Seeing guards chasing after healers and harpers was very interesting. Especially guards who did not wish to follow their particular orders. I could just imagine Barndy's consternation. 'Arrest the Masterharper, Lord Tolocamp? Now, how could I do such a thing? The healers, too? Are they not needed more in their own Hall right now than here?'

There was a brief scuffle as Tirone barged through the half-hearted attempt to thwart him. I suppose words were exchanged between the guards and the others, but no one truly interfered with those departing, and Master Tirone led them all down on to the road at a good pace.

Our path had already taken us across the roadway, and their steps would cover our footprints in the dust. I continued my awkward pace and wondered if my father even noticed the passing of the drudges. Sim and the other two had reached the perimeter, and Theng was looking with some disgust at their burdens. He had come hastily out of his little hut, but then he identified the basket holding the noon meal of the guard contingent and relaxed.

I began to worry about Master Capiam immured in the

camp when he really ought to remain in his Hall, no matter what he had said to Master Tirone.

'If you go past the perimeter, Master Capiam, you will not be permitted back.'

'If there is more than one way into the Hold, is there only one past the perimeter?' he asked me flippantly. 'I'll see you later, Lady Nerilka.'

I was relieved to think he was right. I was close enough to the dip in the roadway to see the encampment, and the men and women, well back of the guarded zone, waiting patiently for the food.

'Here now, Master Capiam.' Theng came up, alarmed to see the resolution in the Masterhealer's stride. 'You can't go in there without staying—'

'I don't want this medicine heaved about, Theng. Make sure they understand it's fragile.'

I turned to one side, pretending to ease the weight of the demijohn. Theng knew me well enough to raise a commotion if he recognized me.

'I can do that much for you,' Theng replied. He placed the demijohn to one side of the bales, then yelled down to the waiting men and women. 'This is to be handled carefully, and preferably by a healer. Master Capiam says it's medicine.'

I wanted to tell Capiam that I would see that the medicine was given to the appropriate people, but I dared not get too close to Theng, who was now making sure that Master Capiam went back where he belonged. I took the opportunity and walked quickly down the slope to the waiting people.

'Nah, then, Master Capiam,' Theng was saying as I made good my escape, 'you know I can't allow you close contact with any of your craftsmen.'

I was immensely relieved that Theng intervened at that point. It was presumptuous of me, perhaps, but I felt that Master Capiam ought to remain where he was accessible to drum messages and councils with other Masters, particularly when he and the Masterharper had just pulled their Craftsmen from Fort Hold. As devoted a Craftsman as he was, it was not right that Master Capiam put himself at risk in this wretched camp. Perhaps now that the vaccine was being processed, the internment camp would be dispersed in only a matter of days. It would be a long time, however, before Hold, Hall and Weyr could pick up the skein of routine and unravel the tangle in which the plague had left us.

I had a very selfish reason for being glad that Master Capiam had elected to stay above. I wished to change my identity as well as my Hold. There might be one or two harpers or healers who might recognize me from their attendance at the Hold, but they wouldn't be looking for Lady Nerilka here in the internment camp, surrounded by infection and vulnerable to discomfort as well as to death.

Although she had not said so, Desdra undoubtedly had refused my offers of assistance because she knew that young ladies of Hold Blood did not engage in such activities on a public basis. She probably considered me a feckless, trivial person and perhaps I was: some of my recent thoughts and decisions could have been considered petty. But I did not consider that I was sacrificing my high rank and position. I thought, rather, that I was putting myself in the way of being useful, instead of immured in a Hold, protected and unproductive, wasting my energy on trivia like sewing for my stepmother. Such a 'suitable occupation' for a girl of my rank could so easily be undertaken by the least drudge from the linen rooms.

These thoughts fleeted through my head as I kept up the awkward gait I had assumed – ironic, as Hold girls were taught to take such tiny steps that they appeared to float across the floor. I had never quite mastered that skill. I followed the men and women who had brought the baskets to the perimeter. Now I could see that most of them wore harper knots. One man wore the colours of the River Hold, and another of the Sea Hold. Travellers trapped on their way to seek help from Tolocamp? The path turned off into the copse, where I could now see that rude shelters had been erected. We had been indeed fortunate that the weather had been so clement, for the third month was generally blustery, often blizzardy, and freezing cold. Each open fire in its ring of stones wore either spit or kettle iron. Was this where my restorative soups had gone? Then I realized that those huddled blankets or hides about each fire had the grey complexions and lacklustre expressions of convalescents.

One larger shelter, its sides made of an odd assortment of materials, was set to one edge of the copse, and from it issued a chorus of rasping coughs and groans that labelled it the main infirmary. It was towards this that the demijohn of fellis was being taken. Those carrying the baskets of food were beginning to distribute bread to those at the fires. Three women began to sort the vegetables and meat scraps into kettles. The silence was the worst of the scene.

I hastened to the infirmary and was met at the door by a tall, unshaven healer. 'Fellis, herbs – what have you?' he asked eagerly.

'Tussilago. Lady Nerilka made it fresh last night.'

He grimaced and took the demijohn from me. 'It's heartening to know not everyone there agrees with the Lord Holder.'

'He's a hypocritical coward.'

The healer raised eyebrows in surprise. 'Young woman, it is unwise to speak of your Lord Holder in that fashion, no matter what the provocation.'

'He is not my Lord Holder,' I replied, meeting his stare unflinchingly. 'I have come to help. I have a firm grounding in the properties of herbs and their preparation. I . . . helped Lady Nerilka brew the tussilago. She taught me all I know, and her lady mother now dead at Ruatha. I can nurse and I am not afraid of the plague. All I loved is dead now anyway.'

He put a comforting hand on my shoulder. No one

72

would dare such a familiarity towards the Lady Nerilka, yet I did not find it offensive to be handled. It proved I was a human being.

'You are not alone in that.' He paused for me to fill in my name. 'All right, Rill, I'll take any volunteers right now. My best nurse just succumbed. . . . ' He nodded to a woman, still and white on a pallet of boughs. 'There isn't all that much we can do except relieve the symptoms' – he affectionately patted the container of tussilago – 'and hope there are no secondary infections. It is that which causes death, not the plague itself.'

'There will soon be enough vaccine.' I said it to cheer him, for patently he did not like to be so helpless in the face of this epidemic.

'Where did you hear that, Rill?' He had lowered his voice, and now held my upper arm in a painful grip. All handling is not reassuring.

'It is known. Yesterday the Bloods were inoculated against the disease. More of the serum is being made. You are nearby. . . .'

The man shrugged in bitter acceptance of his situation. 'Nearby, but scarcely a priority.'

The woman struggled in the grip of the fever and flung herself out of her coverings. I went immediately to her side. And that began my first twenty-hour day as a nurse. There were three of us and Macabir, the journeyman healer, to tend the sixty stricken people in that rude infirmary. I never did know how many more the camp held, for the population shifted. Some had arrived on foot as well as by runner, hoping to claim Hold at Fort or assistance from the Halls or the Hold, and left when they realized that they were not permitted to reach their objective. I often wondered how many people actually had obeyed the full quarantine. But we are more populous here in the west than the eastern half of the continent. And the territory under Fort's jurisdiction suffered nowhere near the casualties that Ruatha did. We heard that only Master Capiam's early attendance at South Boll kept the disease from ravaging that province as well. There were those who said that Ratoshigan would have deserved the fate that was dropped on Ruatha and young Lord Alessan.

He was still alive, I learned. But he and his youngest sister were the only survivors of the Bloodline. His losses were more grievous than mine, then. Would his gains be as great?

Though harried, anxious, overworked, underfed, and certainly sleep-deprived, I had never been so happy. Happy? That is a very odd word to use in conjunction with my occupation in the camp, for that day and the next we lost twelve of the sixty lying in the tent, and acquired fifteen in their places. But I was being useful for the first time in my life, and needed, and I was the amazed recipient of the mute gratitude of those I tended. For someone raised as I had been, the experience was a revelation in some rather personal and unpleasant ways as well, for I had never coped with the intimate bodily functions of either man or woman, and now had to attend both. I suppressed my initial revulsion and nausea, cropped my hair even shorter, rolled up my sleeves, and got on with the job. If this was part of it, then it would not be shirked,

I had the added assurance of knowing I was buffered against catching the disease that I nursed, so sometimes Macabir's praise of my courage on this count embarrassed me. Then a journeyman healer walked boldly into the camp bearing sufficient serum to inoculate everyone, and announced that the camp was being struck. The sick would be transported to the Harper Hall, where the apprentice barracks were being cleared to accommodate them. The transients also would find overnight shelter before being sped on their way in the morning. And if they'd be good enough to take along some supplies. . . .

I volunteered, although Macabir repeated his wish for me to take formal training at the Hall. 'You've a natural gift for the profession, Rill.'

74

'I'm far too old to be an apprentice, Macabir.'

'How old is old when you've a right knack with the sick? A Turn and you've done the initial training. Three, and there wouldn't be a healer who'd not be pleased to have you assist him.'

'I'm free now to see more of this continent than one Hold, Macabir.'

He sighed, scrubbing at his lined and weary face. 'Well, keep it in mind if you find travel palls.'

Chapter Seven

3.19.43–3.20.43

I LEFT IN THE EARLY EVENING LIGHT, with a rough map to show me the way to three northern holds, quite close to the Ruathan border, where serum and other urgent medicinal supplies were needed. Macabir tried to persuade me to wait until the morning, but I reminded him that there was light enough with the full moon to travel those open roads, and the need was immediate. I wanted to take no chance that Desdra or someone from the Hold might recognize Lady Nerilka, dishevelled and worn though she was.

I rode past Fort Hold, without so much as a glance to see if Tolocamp was at his window, past the cot ranks and the beastholds, and wondered if any one of the many people with whom I had spent my life up until three days ago saw me pass. Had anyone, indeed, with the exception of Anella and my sisters, missed me?

My folly was that I was more fatigued than I had suspected before the routine of nursing was stripped from me. I dozed half a dozen times in the saddle. Fortunately the runner was an honest beast and, once set on the track, continued for lack of other instruction. Reaching the first hold by midnight, I managed to inject the household before I collapsed. They let me sleep myself out, for which I berated the good lady when she fed me a huge breakfast at dawn, but she merely replied that the other holds knew I was coming and that was certainly better than wondering if they'd been totally forgotten.

So I rode on, arriving at the second hold by mid-morning. They insisted that I stay for a meal, for I looked so tired and worn. They knew that there was no sickness at my final stop, and they were anxious for all the news I could give them. Until my arrival, they had been kept informed only by drum messages from my next stop, High Hill Hold, right on the border of Ruatha.

I finally admitted to myself that I was on my way to Ruatha. I had been unconsciously drawn towards that destination for many Turns, but had been thwarted so often by circumstance. Now, I reasoned to myself as I continued on the next leg of my journey, I had a skill to bring to that most tragic of Holds. Only dragonriders had been in to Ruatha Main Hold, and rumours of the devastation were horrific. Well, I could nurse the sick, manage any area of Hold activity, and do what I could to expiate the guilt I still carried for the untimely deaths of my mother and sisters.

I was also beginning to realize that the plague had struck with a fine disregard for rank, health, age and usefulness. It is true that the very young and the very old were more vulnerable, but the epidemic had claimed so many in the prime of life with so much living left to be done. If it suited me to clothe my action in the fine garb of sacrifice or expedience, as long as I performed the services required what matter the motives, hidden or open?

Arriving at High Hill Hold in the early afternoon, I was set immediately to work to stitch a long gash sustained by one of the holder's sons, despite my protestations that I was only a messenger. Their healer had gone down to Fort Hold when the news had been drummed out of Ruatha. Since I could tell them nothing of a man named Trelbin, they sadly realized that he, too, must be dead.

Lady Gana said she was capable of dealing with minor cuts, but treating this wound was beyond her ability. Well, I had assisted at sufficient surgeries of this nature, so that I felt more confident in this instance than she obviously was.

Stitching a seam on fabric, which does not complain and cannot squirm, is quite a different matter from repairing ragged and uneven flesh. I had sufficient fellis and numbweed among the supplies I carried to ease the boy's discomfort and I sincerely hoped that my stitches held. Lady Gana announced herself impressed when I had finished.

Later I explained about the serum, then injected everyone except their high-hold shepherds, who never came near enough to populated areas to catch an infection. Lady Gana was still not quite sure that the wind did not carry the disease, so she insisted that I tell her exactly how to cope with it. I know she did not believe me when I told her that death was not caused by the disease itself, but by secondary infections occurring in a patient already weakened. That is why I couldn't really admit that I was not a trained healer. I would undo all the good I had done. Whether I was trained or not, my information was accurate.

Bestrum and Gana then sadly related that a son and daughter accompanied by a servant had gone to the Ruathan Gather and they had had no word from them. They obviously hoped that I was bound for Ruatha.

Bestrum was laboriously sketching a map for me to follow when we were interrupted by excited shouts and cheers. Leaning out the windows we saw a blue dragon, curiously laden, settle to the ground. All of us rushed out to greet him.

'My name is M'barak, Arith's rider, of Fort Weyr. I come in search of more apprentice-blown glass bottles.' The lad grinned engagingly as he pointed to the dragon's burdens. 'Have you any you can spare Ruatha?'

However young, he had to be given the courtesies due

a dragonrider, so over klah and some of Lady Gana's excellent wine cake he told us that runnerbeasts also were dying of the plague, and needed to be inoculated. Bestrum and Gana took some pride in remarking that they had received their injections only that morning, and indicated me. I almost laughed as M'barak blinked, for I know he had assumed I was of this hold. Although I still wore coarse trousers and felt boots, Macabir had given me healer tunic and surcoat against the rigours of travel. I didn't look like a proper healer and I at least knew it, if the kind holders did not.

'Were you just going back to the Healer Hall now?' M'barak began. 'Because, if you happened to be handy with runnerbeasts, you'd be of tremendous use right now at Ruatha. I can take you' – his eyes twinkled with mischievous delight – 'and save you a long and tedious journey. Tuero could drum the Hall to tell 'em where you are. It's just getting people up to Ruatha right now, people who've been injected and aren't afraid of the plague. You're not afraid, are you?'

I only shook my head, a bit shocked at the way my pulses had leaped and my heart skipped at this unexpected invitation to go where I desperately wanted to be. During Suriana's lifetime, Ruatha had been the lodestone for my only chance of some happiness and freedom. I had freed myself of Fort Hold's Blood yoke and was now equally free to go to Ruatha, especially now that I had been given what was tantamount to an invitation. It would be a Ruatha sadly changed from the Hold Suriana had described, but I would be of more use there now, especially going as Rill, not as Lady Nerilka. It was employment and purpose I sought, wasn't it?

'If it's someone good with runners you need, I've two men here spending their waking hours carving scrimshaw for lack of something to do till spring comes in earnest,' Bestrum said expansively. 'Rill jabbed 'em with the rest of us this morning, so they've no call to fear going to Ruatha.'

So it was arranged. As the two beasthandlers, brothers sharing the same phlegmatic temperament and stolid build, collected their necessaries, Gana kindly fetched out a heavy cloak against the biting cold of *between*. She bustled about with her drudges, organizing provisions for three more mouths as well as collecting three great apprentice-blown glass jars, which M'barak and I had to arrange so as not to crack together on Arith.

This was by no means my first contact with a dragon, but certainly it was the most extended and personal. Dragons have a warm, very smooth, soft hide, which leaves a spicy smell on your hands. Arith rumbled a lot, though M'barak assured me that it didn't mean he was annoyed with his unusual burden. We padded the great glass bottles; Fort had more than its share of these apprentice efforts, although I cannot remember what Mother did with them.

I made a final check on the boy's wound, but it looked unchanged and he was fast asleep, a smile on his face from the fellis. Then I took my farewell of Bestrum and Gana, who, though I had known them only a few hours, were profuse in their good wishes. I told them that I would ask about their children and the servant, and send back word. Gana knew there was slight hope, but the offer gave her comfort.

When Bestrum gave me a heave to the dragon's back, I thumped into place behind M'barak's slight but straight body and hoped I didn't hurt Arith. The two brothers got aboard with less fuss, and it was comforting to know that there were two behind me to fall off before I would be in danger.

Arith executed a little run before he jumped skywards, then his fragile-looking, transparent wings took the first mighty sweep downwards. It was the most exhilarating experience I had ever had, and I envied dragonriders anew as Arith's strong wings carried us further aloft. I needed the cloak as well as the buffer of warm bodies in front and behind me.

M'barak must have known how I was feeling, for he turned his head and gave me a wide pleased grin. 'Hold on now, Rill, we're going *between*,' he yelled. At least, that's what I thought he must have said as the wind tore his voice away.

If flying dragonback is exhilarating, going *between* is the essence of terror. Blackness, nothingness, a cold so intense my extremities ached, and only the knowledge that riders and dragons experienced the same thing daily with no ill effect kept me from screaming in fear. Just as I was sure I would suffocate, we were sunstruck again as Arith brought us by that unique draconic instinct to our destination. Then I had far more to concern me than that fleeting passage through black *between*.

I had never been to Ruatha Hold, but Suriana had sent me innumerable sketches of the establishment and had described its amenities time and again. The great Hold, carved from the living rock of the cliff-face, could not be altered physically, but somehow it was completely unlike Suriana's drawings. She had told me of the pleasant air about the Hold, of the hospitality and warmth and friendliness so different from the cool, detached formality of Fort. She had explained how many people, family and otherwise, were constantly in and out of the Hold. She had described the meadows, the racing flats, the lovely fields down to the river. She had not lived to describe the huge burial mounds or the charnel circle of blackened earth, the litter of broken travel-wagons and personal effects that were scattered up the roadstead that had once been graced by Gather stalls, bright with banners and people and barter.

I was stunned, and only peripherally aware that the phlegmatic brothers were also shocked by the view. Mercifully, M'barak was a tactful young man and said nothing as Arith glided past the desolate Hold. I did see one encouraging sight: five people seated in the court, obviously soaking up the afternoon sun.

'Two dragons now, Brother,' the man directly behind me said with great satisfaction.

Looking ahead, I could see that a great bronze dragon was depositing passengers at the wide entrance to the beasthold. The bronze took off as Arith hurtled across the ploughed fields. We could see sun gleaming on his hide and wings, and then he just disappeared. Arith settled down in exactly the same spot the bronze had occupied.

'Moreta,' M'barak called, gesturing eagerly. The tall woman with short, curly blonde hair turned back to him. The Fort Weyrwoman was the last person I expected to encounter at Ruatha.

I shall always remember that I had that opportunity to see Moreta again and at that particular moment in her life, when her face was tinged with sun and an inner serenity that I was not to understand until much later. She had, of course, been at Fort Hold in her capacity of Weyrwoman since she had assumed that responsibility on Leri's retirement. But these were infrequent visits – on state occasions – so although I had been in the same Hall with her we had never actually spoken together. I had had the impression that she was shy or reticent but, then, Tolocamp did so much talking in that ponderous way of his that I doubt she'd have had a chance to speak.

'Hurry up!' M'barak's voice hauled me away from my impressions of that moment. 'I need help with these silly bottles and I've people here who say they can handle runners. And we've got to hurry because I have to prepare for the Fall. F'neldril will skin me if I'm late!'

Two other men and a slim, dark-haired girl moved out of the shadows to help. I knew Alessan on the instant and supposed the girl must be his surviving sister, Oklina. The other man wore Harper blue. The brothers dismounted quickly, and M'barak and I handed down first the provisions and then the great bottles, none of which had suffered any travel damage.

'If you'll slip down, Moreta can mount,' M'barak suggested, with a grin of apology for his haste.

So, for the first time, I traded places with Moreta. I would have liked to sustain the contact then, for she had a manner about her that made one want to get to know her better. She appeared considerably less aloof than she had seemed in the Hold. As Arith began his preparatory little run, Moreta did look back over her shoulder. But it couldn't have been at me.

I turned and saw that Alessan had shaded his eyes to watch until the dragon went *between*. Then he smiled, his welcome taking me in along with the two brothers, and held out his hand in the friendliest way. 'You've come to help us with the runners? Was M'barak frank about what is needed in ruined Ruatha?'

At first I thought he sounded bitter, but came to understand that he did not hide from the grim realities of his situation. He ever had a wry sense of humour, but Suriana, preparing me for my long-expected visit to Ruatha, had warned me of that. What would she think of her foster sister coming here like this?

'Bestrum sent us, Lord Alessan, with his condolences and greetings,' said the more grizzled of the two men. 'I'm Pol; my brother's Sal. We like runners better nor other beasts.'

Alessan turned his smiling light-green eyes to me, and all that Suriana had told me about him rattled through my head. But the sketches that she had also sent did not do him justice, or else he had changed dramatically from that young and rather reckless-looking young man. There was now considerably more character about the eyes and mouth, and an ineffable sadness, despite the smile of his greeting – a sadness that would fade, but never leave. He was thin, had been fever-gaunt; the broad bones of his shoulders pushed through his tunic, and his hands were rough, calloused, cracked and pricked, more like a common drudge's than a Lord Holder's.

'I'm Rill,' I said, to bring myself back to the present

83

and to guard against unexpected queries. 'I have always managed runners. I've some experience in healing and concocting all kinds of medicine from herbs, roots and tubers. And I've brought some supplies with me.'

'Would you have anything for the racking cough?' the girl asked, her huge dark eyes shining. Such a shining could scarcely be for me or for the provision of cough syrup, but I did not know until much later how these people had spent the unusual hour that had just ended moments before we arrived.

'Yes, I do have,' I said, hefting my saddlebags packed with the bottles of tussilago.

'Holder Bestrum wanted to know if his son and daughter live,' Pol asked bluntly, shifting uncomfortably from foot to foot while his brother looked anywhere but at Lord Alessan.

'I'll look at the records,' the harper said gently, but we had all noticed the shuttering expression that dampened the smile in Alessan's eyes. And Oklina had given a little gasp. 'I'm Tuero,' the harper went on, smiling to reassure us all. 'Alessan, what's the order of business now?'

And so Tuero deftly turned our thoughts to the future, away from the sorrowful past. Shortly we had no time for anything, past or future. The present consumed us.

Alessan quickly explained what had to be done. First, the few patients still remaining in the Main Hall infirmary had to be moved to quarters on the second level of the Hold. Then the Hall must be scrubbed thoroughly with redwort solution. He looked beyond me, from whom he could expect assistance at such a task, to Pol and Sal.

'We must make sufficient serum to inoculate runner-beasts.' He turned and gestured towards the pasture. 'We will take blood from those that survived the plague.'

Pol stopped mid-nod and glanced at Sal. I must admit that I was stunned by the look of the runnerbeasts. Many were weedy, with light bones and high haunches, rather thin-necked and far too gaunt to bear any resemblance to the sturdily conformed, rugged, firm-fleshed beasts that had been the pride of Ruatha Hold. Some were no more than great walking bone-racks.

Alessan noticed our consternation. 'Most of the beasts that my father bred died of the plague.' His tone was matter-of-fact and we took our cue from it. 'Those that I had bred for speed over short distances turned out to be resilient and came through, as did some of the cross-breds that our guests had brought.'

'Oh, the pity of it, the pity of it,' Pol murmured, shaking his grizzled head. His brother did the same.

'Oh, I shall breed fine strong beasts again. Would you know my handler, Dag?' Alessan asked the brothers. They both brightened and nodded with more enthusiasm. 'He'd some of the mares in foal and a young stallion up in the hill meadows. They survived, so I've some of the old basic stock to breed from.'

'Good to hear, lord, good to hear.' Sal's words were directed more to the runners than to Alessan.

'But' – Alessan grinned apologetically to the two men – 'before we can start collecting blood for the serum, we have to have a clean and totally uncontaminated place in which to work.'

Pol began rolling up his sleeve. 'There isn't much my brother and I wouldn't do to help you, lord. We've scrubbed before, we can scrub again.'

'Good, then,' Alessan said with a grin. 'Because, if we don't do it right the first time, journeywoman Desdra will make us do it all over again until we have! She'll be here tomorrow to check on our labours.'

When we reached the courtyard before the Hold door, Tuero, a man named to me as Deefer, five fosterlings, and four of the convalescent farm-holders were constructing a strange device from cartwheels.

'We'll have several of these centrifuges with which to separate the miracle serum from the blood,' Alessan told us. The brothers nodded as if they knew exactly what he was talking about, though some confusion and surprise showed on Sal's face.

Oklina met us in the Hall, leading out the procession of drudges with their buckets of hot water, cleaning-rags and brooms. She carried containers which I recognized as those generally used to store the strong cleaning fluid. We all rolled up our sleeves and I noticed that Alessan's hands were red already, though there was only a fainter tinge of red on his upper arms. Then we all set to scrubbing.

We scrubbed until the glowbaskets were lit, scrubbed even as we munched with meatrolls in one hand and tried to ignore the faint taste of astringency that the overpowering aroma of redwort invariably gave to anything in its vicinity. We scrubbed until the first sets of glowbaskets had to be replaced.

Alessan had to shake me several times before I left off the scrubbing motion and realized that the others had quit this labour. 'You're all but asleep and still scrubbing, Rill,' he said, but he spoke with such a kind sort of raillery that I gave him a rueful grin.

I had barely enough energy to follow Oklina up the stairs to the first-storey inner room that she assigned me. I remembered that I bade her goodnight as I closed the door. I knew I should plan a few words to say to Desdra on her arrival the next day, so that she would not expose me as Tolocamp's mutinous daughter, but the moment I fell across the bed I fell asleep.

Chapter Eight

3.21.43–3.22.43

I WOKE, STARTLED, as people do at finding themselves in a strange place, and had to reassure myself that I was not back in my room at Fort Hold. It was silence that I heard so palpably, a silence that confused me more than did the slightly strange surroundings. Then I isolated the difference – no drums at all. I rose and dressed, and began my first full day at Ruatha.

I was in the Hall, drinking klah and eating a quick breakfast of porridge, when Desdra arrived on Arith. We all went out at the commotion, for the little dragon was once again draped with many bottles, the large apprentice size and the smaller ones for the all-important serum.

I had no chance to speak with Desdra, for Alessan singled me out with the two brothers and took us off to the field to begin the next step in making the serum.

Either the animals were apathetic from their recent illness or they had been well handled, so we were each able to lead in two at a time. A second and third trip filled all the stalls in the beasthold, then Alessan demonstrated how to draw blood from the neck vein. All the creatures kindly submitted to this bloodletting. Sal and I began to work as a team, and when I saw that he had little stomach

87

for inserting the needlethorn I took over that job as he held each runner's head.

It was full noon before we had finished with the twenty-four beasts. After each drawing, the blood was decanted into the great apprentice jars, then transported to the Hall and secured on to the cartwheel centrifuges. Though I was not the only one dubious about the device, much less the process, Desdra's attitude towards the manufacture was so reassuringly calm that we didn't question anything. As soon as she had checked the fastenings, she motioned the crews of men to begin spinning the wheels. The men changed places at the flywheels frequently, always keeping the speed of the whirling at the same pace. I thought briefly what a mess one loose jar could make of the Hall, and all our cleaning to be done again, and then decided that such ruminations were unsuited to the general air of hope and industry in Ruatha.

Oklina passed among us then, with a hearty soup and warm bread rolls. When Desdra finally joined us, many of us crammed at one long trestle table and others leaning against the walls, she explained the urgency of our monumental task. Only a mass and instantaneous inoculation of threatened runners would prevent the plague from recurring. Everyone in Ruatha Hold would have some part in this enterprise, for the plague must not be permitted to have a second chance at decimating the continent. The news created a hushed silence.

While awaiting the results of the first batch, Pol, Sal and I went back to the beasthold to see how our patients did. Dag was already mixing them a hearty meal of warmed bran with a fortified wine and some herbs, which the old handler said would strengthen the new blood. Then we groomed them well, taking the mud and burrs from their tails and manes.

Despite his splinted right leg, Dag worked right along with us. What he couldn't do for himself was accomplished by his grandson, a rascally, impudent, possessive lad named Fergal. He seemed suspicious of everyone, especially of Alessan when the lord came to see how the beasts had stood up to the bloodletting. The only person whose bidding Fergal would ever do without quibble was Oklina. Every other order he contested with questions that were sheer impudence. Dag, he adored. Obviously he thought the bandy-legged little runner-handler could do no wrong. But, for all his insolence, Fergal was patently dedicated to the beasts. A very pregnant mare took most of his caring; swollen though she was in the last days of gestation, she had a way of cocking her head, ears pricking forward and whuffling at Fergal in a manner I thought most ingratiating.

'The first batch should be done soon,' Alessan announced suddenly.

I was amused that, of the group working with the beasts, Fergal and I were the only ones eager to see the result. Pol and Sal ensconced themselves on bales for a comfortable chat with Dag, politely declining the invitation to see the finished serum.

What startled me was the odd straw-yellow fluid that was the product of this centrifugal process. By the time we got to the Hall, Desdra was already drawing it from one jar, explaining how this should be done without stirring up the darker residue. Under her direction, we tentatively began to imitate her, drawing the clear fluid from the jar, placing it in the glass bottles, using a clean needlethorn with each insertion to reduce the possibility of contamination. Ruthlessly, Desdra employed everyone at the Hall at this task, even three of the strongest convalescents, constantly moving amongst us to oversee the task.

'We should have more bottles this afternoon,' Tuero told us. He meant to be cheerful but was rewarded by groans from all the workforce. 'M'barak said he'd pass the word of our need during Fall.'

'How much of this junk do we gotta have?' Fergal asked. He glanced out towards the fields where his beloved runners grazed.

89

'Enough to inoculate the mares and foals of the remaining herds in Keroon, Telgar, Ruatha, Fort, Boll, Igen and Ista,' Alessan said. I stifled a groan at the quantities that would be required.

'Ista doesn't breed runners. It's an island,' Fergal said belligerently.

'It suffered the plague, man and beast,' Fuero said when Alessan did not reply. 'Keroon and Telgar are also producing the serum, so Ruatha doesn't have to do it all.'

'Ruatha has that much, at least, to give Pern,' Alessan added, as if no other comments had been made. 'We will ensure that the best possible serum comes from our beasts. Let us return to our tasks.'

And so we persevered. Those who had not fully recovered were put to sitting at sinks to scrub glassware or securely stopper the serum-bottles and insert them in reed holders. The youngest became messengers or, in pairs, carefully carried crates of serum down to the cool rooms.

My job was bleeding runners. It was almost a relief to leave the pervading stench of redwort to bring my patient-victim back to the field and collect another one. At least I had some fresh air. Dag had started marking the bled ones with paint so we wouldn't inadvertently get two lots from the same beast. None of them was strong enough for that. My frequent walks also gave me a chance to observe ruined Ruatha, as Alessan called it. I could see that only a little time and effort would be required to put a lot of the ruin to rights, and I worked out the strategy going to and fro, planning all that I would do if I had the right to meddle in Ruathan affairs. A harmless enough pastime, to be sure.

The drums had begun mid-morning, telling us what quantities were needed and which dragonriders would collect what amounts. Alessan explained that the quantities had to be listed accurately, but he really couldn't spare Tuero to listen to drum codes.

'Then have Rill do it,' Desdra said bluntly.

'Can you understand drum messages, Rill?' Alessan asked, somewhat surprised. I had been taken so unaware that I couldn't answer. I had even begun to think that Desdra had not recognized Tolocamp's daughter in grimy, sweaty, short-haired Rill.

'And probably the codes as well, isn't that right, Rill?' Desdra was quite ruthless, but at least she did not explain to anyone how she knew so much about my unmentioned skills. 'She can fill serum-bottles between messages. She needs a bit of sit-down time. She's been going full pelt for some days now.'

I took that to mean that Desdra approved of my labours here and at the internment camp and was permitting me my whimsy. Fortunately, not even Alessan questioned how a drudge who had risen to volunteer healer understood such arcane matters. But I was indeed grateful for the chance to sit down. How Alessan kept up his level of energy I do not know. I could see why Suriana had admired as well as adored him. He deserved respect, and he had mine for new reasons at every turn. I could also perceive that he was driven. Somehow, despite all the brutal odds against him, Alessan was going to restore Ruatha Hold, repeople its vacant holds, restock its empty fields. I wanted to stay on here, and help him.

I was also discovering that, once back in a formal Hall, I automatically assumed familiar responsibilities, such as ordering drudges to tasks or explaining how to do a job more efficiently. Fortunately, no one questioned my right to do so when it was all in the best interest of the work at hand.

Despite a deceptively frail appearance, Oklina worked as hard as her brother, but the sheer press of her obligations appalled me, who had always had sisters to ease burdens. Whenever I could, I lent her a hand. She wasn't a pretty girl, which the uncharitable might say was one reason I related to her so easily, for the dark complexion and strong features that became a man suited her no better than my

91

family resemblance suited me. But she was an exceptionally graceful young woman, with a charming smile and great, dark, expressive eyes in which lurked a sort of secret bemusement. I often caught her gazing towards the northwest and wondered if she had fallen in love with some young man. She would make an excellent holder's wife, young though she was, and I devoutly hoped that Alessan would not require her to remain at Ruatha, but would settle her with a kind and generous man. Ruatha might be poverty-stricken now, but the prestige of the Bloodline was still undisputed. Nor would this altruistic labour on the serum, so willingly undertaken by Alessan and Oklina, reduce them in the estimation of their peers.

And so we worked on, turning from one urgent and necessary task to another, ladling a quick cup of soup from the pot simmering on the main hearth, or chewing from a hunk of fresh bread in a free hand and a spare moment. From somewhere, fresh fruit had appeared – one of the dragonriders was dropping off supplies. Why ripe melon slices would cause Oklina's eyes to tear, I could not then fathom. I doubted that she was so moved by the thoughtfulness behind the gift. Then I noticed that Alessan regarded the fruit with a soft smile of reminiscence, but he was off to work again so quickly, bread in one hand, the melon slice in the other, that I could have been wrong. Then another message came in, and I had to listen to record the message accurately.

Time had lost all order in the press of work. On my third day at Ruatha, all but a few of us had gone outside to eat a delayed and well-deserved evening meal when suddenly Alessan, Desdra and Tuero, consulting the maps, lists and charts, gave out whoops of exultation.

'We've done it, my loyal crew!' Alessan shouted. 'We've got enough! And enough over the requirement to take care of any spillage and breakage in dispatching. It's wine all round! Oklina, take Rill and get four flasks from my private store.'

He tossed her a long slim key, which she caught deftly in mid-air. She grabbed my hand and, laughing with delight, hauled me to the kitchen and then on down to the stores, beyond the cold room.

'He is really pleased, Rill. He rarely parts with bottles of his own store.' She giggled again. 'He guards them for a special purpose.' Then her charming little face saddened. 'And I hope he will again,' she added cryptically. 'He must soon in any case. Here we are.'

When she had unlocked the narrow door and showed me the racked flasks and wineskins, I gasped in astonishment. Even in the dim light from the glowbasket down the corridor, I could see the distinctive Benden flask. Quickly I dusted off a label.

'It *is* Benden white,' I cried.

'You've had Benden white wine?'

'No, of course not.' Tolocamp would not have approved of his daughters drinking rare vintages; the foxy Tillek pressings were good enough for us. 'But I've heard about it,' I managed to giggle. 'Is it really as good as they say?'

'You can judge for yourself, Rill.'

She locked the door again, then relieved me of half the burden.

'Did you finish your training at the Healer Hall, Rill?'

'No, no.' Somehow I could not lie to Oklina even if it meant demeaning myself in her eyes. 'I volunteered to help nurse, as I wasn't needed any longer in my own Hold.'

'Oh, did your husband die of the plague?'

'I have none.'

'Well, Alessan will see to that. That is, of course, if you wish to stay on in Ruatha. You've been such a help, Rill, and you seem to understand a great deal about Hold management. I mean, we shall have to start all over again; so many of our people died. There are many holds empty and, while Alessan is going to approach the holdless in hopes that some are suitable, I'd rather have

93

a few people about us whom we already know and trust. Oh, Rill, I'm putting this so badly. But Alessan asked me to sound you out about staying on here at Ruatha. He has great respect for you. You have been such a help. Tuero' – Oklina giggled again – 'plans to stay, no matter how he and Alessan go on about the salary and perks.'

That discussion had been running between harper and Lord Holder whenever they passed each other or worked on a common chore. Tuero had come to the Gather with other harpers to assist the Hold's regular harper, another victim, as were Tuero's companions. I couldn't imagine Ruatha Hold without Alessan and Tuero bickering in the most amiable fashion.

When we returned to the Main Hall, the men had stacked some of the cartwheels and the large jars back against the wall. Alessan and Tuero were clearing space on the trestle table, where we had been consuming our hasty meals. Dag and Fergal came up from the kitchen with the stew; Deefer brought plates and cutlery; Desdra had an armful of bread loaves and a huge wooden bowl full of fruit and cheeses, including the one forwarded by Lady Gana. I wouldn't have thought that that would have lasted past my bringing it here. Follen arrived with the cups and the cork-pull.

Outside I could hear the subdued revelry of the others who had now been released from their unremitting labours of the past two days.

So it was only the eight of Alessan's loyal crew, an odd assortment to sit down at any table for any meal, but the knowledge of an almost impossible task completed in good time made companions of us all, even Fergal. He refused a cup of wine with an insolence that I'm certain Alessan excused only because the boy had worked so hard. I'd wager that Fergal was as knowledgeable about such restricted treats as anyone else here. Fergal's sort is born knowing. In spite of his impudence and suspicious nature, I did like the boy.

That dinner was a very happy event for me. Alessan

had taken the seat next to me, and I found his proximity strangely agitating. I tried to avoid touching him, but we were rather crowded on the benches, companionably so for everyone else. Since he was close to me, his arm resting on the table touched mine, occasionally his thigh brushed mine, and he grinned at me when Tuero said something particularly amusing. My heart raced, and I knew that my answering laugh was a little high and foolish. I was tired, I expect, over-reacting to the success we were celebrating, and very much unused to the fine white Benden wine.

Then Alessan leaned against me deliberately, touching my forearm with his fingertips. My skin tingled.

'What's your opinion of the Benden, Rill?'

'It's made me giddy,' I replied quickly so that, if he noticed my unusual behaviour, he would know the reason, even though I wished to do nothing to lower myself in his good opinion.

'We all need to relax tonight. We all deserve it.'

'You more than anyone else, Alessan.'

He shrugged and looked down at his cup, his fingers idly twisting it around by the stem. 'I do what I must,' he said, speaking in a low voice. The others were involved in an argument.

'For Ruatha,' I murmured.

He looked at me, mildly surprised at my rejoinder, his strange green-flecked eyes for once candid. 'That's perceptive of you, Rill. Have I been such a hard task-master?'

'Not for Ruatha's sake.'

'This' – he waved his hand at the cartwheels and empty jars – 'has not been for Ruatha's sake.'

'Oh, but it has. You said so yourself. Ruatha can do this much for Pern.'

He gave a slightly embarrassed laugh. But his smile was kind, and I think he was pleased.

'Ruatha will be herself again! I know it!' It was safer to talk about Ruatha's future.

95

There was an odd expression in his eyes. 'Then, Oklina spoke to you? You'll consider staying on with us?'

'I would like to very much. The plague left me holdless.'

His warm strong hand closed on mine, squeezing lightly in gratitude. 'And do you have any special requirements, Rill, to cement our relationship?' There was a real gleam in his eye now as he tilted his head towards Tuero.

His question had come up so unexpectedly that I'd had no time to think about anything beyond the fact that my wish to remain in Ruatha had been granted. I stammered a bit, and then Alessan once again gripped my arm.

'Think about it, Rill, and tell me later. You'll find that I hold fair with my people.'

'I'd be surprised to find aught else.'

He grinned at my vehemence, poured more wine into my cup and his, and so we sealed the agreement in the traditional manner, though I had trouble swallowing past the lump of joy in my throat. Companionably, we finished bread and cheese, listening to the other conversations at the table and to the music outside.

'I wasn't so taken with that Master Balfor, Lord Alessan,' Dag was saying, his eyes on the wine in his cup. He was speaking of the man presently designated to become Beastmaster at Keroon.

'He's not confirmed in the honour,' Alessan said. I could see that he didn't wish to argue the matter right now, especially not in front of Fergal, who was always listening to matters he ought not to hear.

'I'd worry who else might have the rank, for Master Balfor certainly hasn't the experience.'

'He has done all that Master Capiam asked,' Tuero said with an eye on Desdra.

'Ah, it's sad to realize how many good men and women have died.' Dag lifted his cup in a silent toast, which we all drank. 'And sadder to think of the fine bloodlines just wiped out. When I think of the races Squealer will walk away with and no competition to stretch him in a challenge. You say Runel died?' Dag went on. 'Did all his bloodline go?'

'The oldest son and his family are safe in the hold.'

'Ah, well, he's the right one for it. I'll just have a look at that brown mare. She could foal tonight. Come along, Fergal.' Dag picked up his splinted leg and hauled it over the bench. For just a moment, Fergal looked rebellious.

'I'll come with you, if I may,' I said, handing Dag the crutches. 'A birth is a happy moment.' I needed some clean night air to fill my lungs, and clear my head of all that good Benden wine. And I also needed to be away from Alessan's stimulating presence.

My heart was very full and beating erratically. I did not wish to embarrass Alessan with an overflow of gratitude, or any outpouring declaration of loyalty, though I felt both emotions intensely. By a freak of chance I had achieved a miracle: I had been invited to *stay* at Ruatha Hold. Forget that the rationale was prosaic; merely that I was useful, they trusted me, and Ruatha had to rebuild itself. I tried not to let my mind refine upon anything that Oklina had said, much less what Alessan had not. To be able to live at Ruatha was enough. I would be in his company, in the very place that had figured so often in my daydreams, that had been the focus of all happiness. Ruatha could once again be a happy place, and I would have the totally unexpected opportunity to achieve that.

Fergal was with us in a moment. He would not allow me to monopolize his grandfather's company.

The night was clear, the air was fresh, and I could feel spring ascending from the warmer climes. We exchanged nods and smiles with the people sitting before the spit fire and along the cot line. I carried the glowbasket to light our path, though all three of us knew each flag, pebble and dip to the beasthold by now. Fergal ran on ahead.

'If she hasn't foaled by midnight, she's not likely to,' Dag announced. 'We need another colt.'

'Who's the foal's sire?'

'One of old Lord Leef's burthen stallions, so it's a colt

we need to bring the line back. You're staying on with us, are you, Rill?' Dag was generally blunt.

I nodded, unable to answer, the joy and relief at my good fortune too precious to talk about. Dag gave a curt nod of his shaggy head.

'We have need of folk like yourself. Any more where you come from?' He gave me a sly sideways glance.

'Not that I know of,' I replied amiably, hoping to still his curiosity. We hadn't had much time for personal conversations these past two and a half days. Now I saw that I would have to develop an appropriate previous history.

'Not every woman can turn her hand to most chores in Hold and beasthold. Were you in a fair-sized place before the plague?'

'Yes, and it saddens me to think of those I lost.' Maybe that prevarication would suffice. Some ethic in me refused to tell untruths. I sighed. One day the truth surely would come out, but by then I hoped to be so well established at Ruatha that I would be forgiven origin as well as defection.

Fortunately we had arrived at the beasthold. Pol and Sal were there, sitting on bales across from the mare, maintaining a discreet watch. They were soaping a leather harness from the pile of tack collected from Gather detritus as worth saving. Pol handed Fergal a breastplate, green with mould. The boy glanced first at Dag, who nodded, and then grimaced at Pol, but he sat himself down and took up a cloth. Dag and I found bales to sit on and straps to clean.

'Bestrum's second son's looking for cropland,' Pol said out of the contented silence.

'Is he?' Dag asked.

'Strong lad, good worker, got a girl in mind from the next Hold.'

'Think Bestrum will mind after losing the others here?'

'Likes Alessan. Boy'd do better here and Bestrum knows it. Fair man, Bestrum.'

'For sending you and Sal, yes, he is.' Dag kept nodding in approval. Then he looked up at Pol, eyes narrowed in speculation. 'How long can he spare you? I've got all those mares to put to our stallions and this broken leg. . . .'

'You said I'd be helping you, Dag,' Fergal complained, glaring at Pol, who ignored him.

'So you will, lad, but there's more than two of us can handle.'

'Spring comes later in the mountains,' Pol said.

'We be-n't needed a while yet,' Sal added.

'Shall I ask Holder Bestrum when I write to Lady Gana about her children?' I asked.

'That would be kind of you.'

Tuero had established that Lady Gana's daughter had died in the first wave of deaths, nursed by the old servant, who also succumbed. Both were buried in the first of the stark mounds. The son had worked hard helping Norman, the field manager of the racing flats, before they, too, collapsed and died. They lay in the second great mound.

'She be mighty restless,' Sal said, breaking the silence.

Fergal hopped up on the bale, stretching his neck and standing on tiptoe to see.

'She's birthing,' he said with such authority that I had to smother a snicker.

Kindly, none of the men insulted him by looking. But we all heard the mare sink to the deep straw bedding. How clever of animals to improve on humans in this activity. We heard several grunts from the mare, no screams or long ululating cries, no weeping and complaining about her lot, or cursing the man who brought her to this condition.

'Hoofs,' Fergal announced in a low voice. 'Head coming. Normal position.'

I couldn't keep from glancing at Dag, who winked at me, nibbling at a thick straw.

'Ah,' Fergal drawled. 'Just one more push, my beauty, just one little effort on your part . . . ah, there.'

We heard the mare's effort, the rustle and slither on the straw, and simultaneously the suspense was too much for us. We all reached the stall at the same time, peering over the partition as the mare began to lick the placenta from her foal. The head was free and the wet little body began to struggle, the overlong legs kicking with incredible strength for a creature so newly born.

'Hey, you're blocking my view,' Fergal cried. He barged in beside Dag and hung on to the partition edge to pull himself up. 'What is it? What is it?'

The foal was not helping us to sex it – its legs went out at angles to its body. It snorted in disgust at its helplessness. The mare nudged its rear, the little whisk of a tail. It repositioned its legs and made another stab at rising. Its legs did not co-operate, and it gave a high-pitched little squeal of frustration. Its feet scrabbled in the straw as the foal determined to find a purchase and rise. It had skewed about now, and as it flicked its tail in annoyance its sex was revealed. Or, to be more accurate, it revealed that it was not a female.

'A colt foal!' Fergal yelled, having paid more attention to that critical detail while we were all enchanted by the creature's sturdy independence. He flipped open the stall door and entered. 'What a marvellous creature you are! What a splendid girl! What a brave mare! What a fine son you have!' Fergal stroked the mare's nose and fondled her ears, his voice rich with approval. Then he began crooning to the colt, gently smoothing the neck to get it used to human touch. The newborn was far too involved in sorting out its legs to worry about any extraneous annoyance.

'He's got a gift for 'em, he has,' Pol told us, sagely nodding his head.

'Delivered three in the hill meadows all by himself after I broke my leg.'

'I'll tell Alessan,' I said.

'The more good news he gets, the better it'll set with him,' Dag said, which struck me, as I walked quickly

100

back up the road, as cryptic for the blunt runner-handler.

When I got back to the Hall, Oklina and Desdra were gone, presumably to bed, for it was after midnight now. Tuero had propped his elbows on the table and was gesturing expansively at Alessan, who had his head down on his arms.

'That's fair enough,' Tuero was saying in a very amiable and conciliatory tone. 'If a harper can't find out – and this harper is very good at finding things out – if a harper can't find out, he doesn't have the right to know. Is that right, Alessan?'

The answer was a long-drawn-out snore. Tuero stared at him for a moment in mixed pity and rebuke, then pushed at the wine-flask under his elbow and sighed in disgust.

'Has he finished it?' I asked, amused at the disappointment on Tuero's long face. His long, crooked-to-the-left nose twitched.

'Yes, it's empty, and he's the only one who knows where the supply is.'

I smiled, remembering my trip with Oklina to the wine-store. 'The foal is a male, a fine strong one. I thought Lord Alessan would like to know. Dag and Fergal are watching to be sure it stands and suckles.' I looked down at the sleeping Alessan, his face relaxed, peaceful. He looked younger, so much less strained. Behind the lids, did those pale green eyes still flicker with their habitual sadness?

'I know I know you,' Tuero said.

'I'm not the sort of person a journeyman harper knows,' I replied. 'Get to your feet, Harper. I can't allow him to sleep in this uncomfortable position, and he needs a proper rest.'

'Not so sure I can stand.'

'Try it.' I am tall, but not as tall as Tuero or Alessan, and not strong enough to shift Alessan's heavy frame by myself. I looped one lax arm over my shoulder and urged

Tuero, who had managed to get upright, to take the other.

Alessan was heavy! And Tuero was not a very able assistant. He had to pull himself up the stairs by the handrail, which I sincerely prayed was firmly secured to the stonework. Fortunately, Alessan's rooms were at the head of the stairs. I hadn't been past the sitting-room, still furnished with the doss-beds and bits and pieces just cast down in the press of other tasks. Tomorrow, or the next day, perhaps we could begin to freshen up the inner Hold.

I gave the heavy fur robe on Alessan's bed a yank, and it tumbled about my feet, briefly hindering us as we manoeuvred Alessan's limp body. He collapsed on to the bed, feet hanging over the edge. Tuero clasped the bedpost, murmuring an apology as the bed-curtain tore a bit from its frame. I tugged off Alessan's boots, loosened his belt, bent his legs upwards, and, with one hand on his hips, gave as mighty a push as I could and managed to get all of his long frame on the bed, on his right side.

'I wish . . .' Tuero began as I covered Alessan with the robe, tucking it in carefully above his shoulders so that if he rolled he would not be cold. He smiled slightly in his sleep and my breath caught. 'I wish. . . .' Tuero stared at me with a suddenly blank face, frowned, and lowered his head to his chest.

'The doss-bed is still in the next room, Harper.' Even with Tuero's drunken help, I doubt I could have assisted him to his room far down the corridor.

'Will you cover me up, too?'

Tuero's request was delivered in such a wistful tone that I had to smile. In two or three lurches, he had followed me into the next room. I picked up the blanket and shook it out. With a sigh of weary gratitude, he lay on his side.

'You're good to a drunken sot of a harper,' he murmured as I covered him. 'One day I'll remem-mmmm. . . .'

102

He was unconscious. Perhaps one day Tuero would remember that it was he who had coined the phrase 'the Fort Hold Horde', which had been joyfully applied to my sisters and me. I suspect it would put a blight on our relationship when he did. But that was really his problem.

Mine was getting into my own bed, and not wishing that there was someone who might care to tuck me in.

Chapter Nine

3.23.43

BRIGHT AND CLEAR, with a promise of spring that was
soon to be blighted in the heart, dawned that momentous
day. Despite our excesses of the night before, or because
of them, we rose rested, and breakfasted early. Everyone
was smiling, including Desdra, who was not much given
to trivial expressions. Details of the day's business were
discussed at the breakfast table. Alessan ran up to the
beasthold to inspect the colt foal, expressing considerable
pleasure in its strength and friskiness. Oklina and I got
the fosterlings and several of the stronger male convalescents to help trundle the apprentice jars up to an
unused beasthold so that some progress could be made
in setting the Main Hall back to the purpose for which it
was intended.

Deefer took others off to see if there might not be a
few plump wherries in the hills; they would make a nice
change from the tough herdbeast meat, the supply of
which was now virtually exhausted.

I made plans in my head, rehearsing suggestions to
present to Alessan tonight. I felt that a week's hard work
would clean up the debris, and he must wish to see the
last of the reminders of that horrible time. Not that we
could do anything to block out the sight of the burial

mounds. Spring would at least bring grass to cloak the muddy prominences. When the earth had settled, we would be able to level them, but that would be some time in the future.

'Dragons!' someone yelled from the Outer Court. We all rushed out to see the spectacle. The first one to land was B'lerion on Nabeth. Oklina's little face filled with joy. Bessera, one of the High Reaches queen riders, on her great beast, settled to the ground behind him. The Court, an ample space, seemed suddenly dwarfed and constricted by the presence of the huge beasts. They looked immensely pleased with themselves, glowing in the bright sunshine. Six more dragons, bronzes all, landed on the roadway.

As Oklina rushed out to B'lerion with his supplies, I could not help but notice the way the bronze rider's face lit up as he slipped down his dragon's side. When she reached him, she halted abruptly to gaze lovingly up at him until, smiling a trifle foolishly himself, he took the serum from her.

I felt a touch on my arm. Desdra stood there with the brace of packaged serum-bottles for me to deliver to a rider. 'Don't stare, Rill. It has been sanctioned.'

'I wasn't staring – not exactly. But she's so young, and B'lerion has quite a reputation.'

'There's a queen egg hardening at Fort Weyr.'

'But Oklina's needed here.'

Desdra shrugged, transferred the serum to my hands, and gave me a bit of a push to call me to attention. I rushed off, but my mind was unsettled. Oklina was so very young, and B'lerion so very charming. Yet Alessan sanctioned the alliance? How odd, when he would need her children as well to secure the Bloodline. Oh, I knew perfectly well that Ruathan women often became queen riders and that Weyrwomen conceived and bore children like any others, though not as prolifically. But I wouldn't fancy such a life. The bond between rider and dragon was too intense, too all-consuming for someone like me.

What I envied in Oklina was the happiness, the rapture in her face as she looked up at B'lerion. Nabeth's rainbow-sparkling eyes were turned on the pair, as if he knew everything that was passing silently between them. Dragons had such powers, I knew. I wasn't certain I would like having someone know exactly what I was thinking all the time. But I supposed dragonriders grew accustomed to it.

No sooner had we recovered our breath from the departure of that dragon contingent than the Fort Weyr queens arrived. Leri, whom I was surprised to see, set old Holth down in the courtyard while Kamiana, Lidora and Haura landed on the roadway. Then S'peren and K'lon arrived. Leri was in great form, joking with Alessan and Desdra, but I noticed that she kept watching Oklina. And so did Holth. So this involvement was of recent origin? Then I remembered my arrival here at Ruatha, a mere three days ago that had the quality of three months, so much had happened in that short space. Alessan had seemed happy; so had Moreta, and Oklina had been positively shining. So was Leri reviewing the situation today?

The Weyr had the right to Search for suitable candidates from any hold, especially when a queen egg was hardening. Oklina was so young, so sweet. I chided myself for criticizing my new Lord Holder. What right had I, save that of a concerned friend? But, then, I was good at seeing the bad side in everything.

Around midday, we had time for a cup of soup and bread. Most of the serum-bottles had been speedily delivered to the messengers – I tried to figure out the logistics of delivery. It took nearly five minutes for a dragon to land. Working as fast as we could, another five minutes were needed to hand the rider the bottles, then three to four minutes for the dragon to become airborne. Although his actual flight time *between* one location and another was a few seconds, it had to take at least half an hour to complete each delivery. With all the holds in the west, South Boll, Crom, Nabol, Fort, what few were occupied in Ruatha, Ista and the western portions of Telgar, the entire complement of each Weyr ought to have been turned out. And there were but eight from the High Reaches, seven from Fort, and six from Ista.

'Don't try to make sense of it, Rill,' Desdra advised me, her wry tone amused. 'It actually can be done if one takes into account unusual draconic abilities.'

Her reference confused me further, but the Istan and Fort contingents of dragons were back for their last consignments. If the dragons looked a bit off-colour, that was to be expected. Going *between* must take a great deal of energy, as did all that landing and taking off. Leri looked exhausted but, then, she was the oldest of the dragonriders at Fort. It was a measure of her dedication to the Weyrs that she undertook such a task.

Suddenly all the queens let out roars of angry protest. The only blue dragon present cringed. Leri looked furious, as did the other queen riders. There seemed to be an intense, if silent, conference among them. Leri signalled me, as the nearest person to her, to take her last consignment from her.

'Take these to S'peren; there's a good girl. He'll deliver.'

I was soon covered in the dust stirred up by Holth's precipitous departure. I think the dragon hadn't so much as cleared the outer wall before she went *between*. A whoosh of cold air made me shudder convulsively. Everyone else had grown grim indeed when there should have been some measure of satisfaction for the completion of a difficult and most unusual task. I walked slowly back to the Hall.

'These can go back to the cool rooms.' Alessan was indicating the remaining crates of serum, the extras prepared against the possibility of breakage. 'We ought to get them over to Keroon Beasthold when the fuss subsides. Whoever becomes Beastcraftmaster will be glad of them. They're sure to discover more abandoned runners in

Keroon or Telgar. There are many untenanted holds there now.'

At that point, Deefer and his team came back, all grinning broadly, each man carrying at least one plump wherry on his back.

'We shall feast tonight. Oklina, Rill, what else can we find in the larder to add to roast wherry? We owe ourselves a real celebration; a proper meal, not another stew, and a swing round with a wineskin.'

There was a general outbreak of cheers and shouts, and offers of assistance to the cooks. The Hall was enthusiastically cleared of its medical detritus, and the long-absent sturdy dinner-tables were hauled, dusty, from their cupboards. They had been so hastily stored after the Gather that some still bore wine- and food-stained cloths. Oklina and I quickly bundled those up and out of sight in the mound of wash.

'I shall be sorry to leave here,' Desdra said to me as she paused in collecting her bits and pieces and her records of the serum manufacture. 'Despite all this' – she gestured at the disorder – 'Ruatha is recovering quickly.'

'You and Master Capiam must come back soon,' Oklina said, her eyes still shining from B'lerion's last visit. 'You'll see what Ruatha should look like, won't she, Rill?'

'Just give me elbow room, and we'll have the place to rights in no time,' I vowed so fervently that Desdra laughed.

Then she winked so that Oklina wouldn't see. 'You were right to come here, Rill. You were never appreciated at your former Hold. And I'd like to apologize for misconstruing your motive in offering your assistance at the Hall. You'd've been a rare, fine help to us there.'

'No, I would not have been allowed,' I said, relieved that Oklina had moved out of earshot. 'Here I am my own person, accepted on the strength of my own endeavours. I can be of use here, especially if Oklina—' I paused, not certain what I meant to say.

108

Desdra cocked one eyebrow, and I quickly corrected any misapprehension she had of high-flown ambitions.

'Oh, don't be ridiculous, Desdra. Despite Ruatha's present state, this is a prestigious Hold for alliance. Alessan's done himself no harm in anyone's eyes to pull out of this disaster with so much dignity. Every Lord Holder with eligible daughters will be courting him assiduously as soon as they can wangle conveyance here.'

'You've sufficient rank, Lady Nerilka.'

'Hush! Rank, to be sure, I *had*.' I emphasized the past tense. 'And little joy of it. I am far more satisfied to be part of Ruatha's future, for I had none of my own at Fort.'

Desdra conceded my point with an open gesture of both hands. 'Is there anyone to whom I should drop a hint of your whereabouts? I shall be most discreet.'

'If you would tell my uncle Munchaun that you have seen me, on your travels, well and happy. He'll reassure my sisters.'

'Campen was worried, too, you know. He and Theskin searched the surroundings for a whole day, certain you had been hurt out gathering herbs.'

I nodded, accepting what she didn't say as well as Campen's attempt.

I remember that I was wondering if we'd ever eradicate the astringent odour of redwort from the Main Hall when Oklina, setting the highly burnished copper ornaments back on the mantel, suddenly cried out and would have fallen had not Desdra, beside her, held her up. Ashenfaced, Alessan burst from the small office that had so recently been Follen's surgery.

'MORRRETTTAAA! Alessan's scream was the anguish of a man already overburdened by grief and loss. He fell heavily to his knees after that one shout, sobs racking his body as he bent over, pounding his fists on the stone, heedless of Follen's attempts to restrain him from doing himself damage.

I couldn't stand those sobs and ran to him, kneeling so

that his already-bloodied fists pummelled my thighs, not cold stone. He gripped my thighs so fiercely I had to bite my lips to suppress a cry, but then he burrowed his head in my lap, convulsed by this grief.

Moreta! What harm could have befallen her at Fort Weyr? I knew that her queen was in the Hatching Ground, surely the safest place in any Weyr.

Alessan's arms encircled my hips, his fingers clawing at my back, as he wrestled with this new and tremendous grief. I clasped him to me as tightly as I could, murmuring inanities, trying to understand what could have happened.

I was aware that Follen and Tuero were standing beside us, but whatever they said was masked by Alessan's hideous, gasping sobs and the scrape of his boots on the stone as his very body tried to escape this new tragedy.

'Whatever it is,' I said, 'let him purge it, for he has not indulged himself with tears until now. What can have happened to Moreta?'

'Whatever', Desdra said, joining them, 'has rendered Oklina unconscious. I don't understand any of this. He's not a rider, nor is she yet.'

We heard a mournful howl, far louder than could have come from the throat of only one watchwher.

'Shards!' Desdra cried.

I looked up at the anguish in her voice and saw B'lerion leaping up the stairs into the Hold, his face totally white, his eyes wild. The greyed dragon beyond him was a terribly altered Nabeth. It was his weird keening we had heard.

'Oklina!' B'lerion cried, trying to find her among us.

'She fainted, B'lerion.' Desdra pointed to the Hall where Oklina's body was stretched out on the table, a servant hovering solicitously by her. 'What has happened to Moreta?'

B'lerion turned haggard tear-filled eyes from Oklina to Alessan, whose sobs as he lay in my arms were as racking as ever, and the bronze rider's whole body sagged as he dropped his head on his chest. Tuero reached out to support him on one side, Follen on the other.

'Moreta went *between*.'

I couldn't quite grasp what he meant. Dragons and riders went *between* so frequently.

'On Holth. Telgar riders defected. She knew Keroon. She made the run. Holth was already tired. She did too much. They both went *between*. And died!'

I held Alessan even tighter then, my own tears mingling with his, my grief as fierce but more for him now than for the valiant Weyrwoman. How could he endure this third ghastly tragedy when he had stood so courageously against the plague, and mourned Suriana far longer than would most men? I burned anew against my father. Why, if there was any justice in the world, was Alessan so grievously assaulted by misfortunes of the most terrible degree while Tolocamp enjoyed health, fortune and fleshly pleasures that he no longer deserved?

I knew then why Alessan's incredible eyes had been shining the day I arrived. I certainly didn't know how Moreta and Alessan had contrived to be lovers. They could not have had much time together at all. On that afternoon, the six had been gone from Ruatha only an hour. Alessan's sanction of Oklina and B'lerion was now more comprehensible if he and Moreta were involved. I was glad that the Weyrwoman had had some joy, for I hadn't liked Sh'gall on those few times I had encountered him. He wasn't likeable, whereas Moreta was. Poor Moreta. Poor, poor Alessan. What could possibly comfort him in this new trial?

Desdra had an answer. She waited until Alessan's sobbing had subsided to shudderings. Then she and Tuero lifted him from my lap. I could not move immediately, so cramped were my legs. But I could and did cushion him against my body as Desdra gently tipped a cup to his lips and told him to drink.

The look in his eyes will always haunt me: lost, totally lost, incredulous of his loss – and so, so sad. He had

111

taken all the draught Desdra had given him, and it was merciful to him as well as to those about him that his eyelids lowered over his ghastly expression as the fellis took instant effect.

There were willing arms to transport him to his quarters, and I willing to sit by him, though Desdra assured me that she had given him enough fellis to keep him asleep until the next day.

'What can we do for him, then, Desdra?' I asked, still shaken by his grief. Tears would not stop coursing down my cheeks.

'My dear Lady Nerilka, if I knew the answer to that, I would be Masterhealer.' She shook her head from side to side, expressing the utter helplessness that I, too, felt to my core. 'It will depend in every degree on what he will allow us to do for him. How cruel this new loss. How horribly, wastefully cruel!'

We undressed him and covered him with the fur. His face was prematurely aged, his eyes shrunken in his head, his lips drawn down, his complexion waxy-white. Desdra felt his pulse and nodded with relief. Then she sat down on the edge of the bed, wearily propping her back against the stead, her hands palms up and limp in her lap.

'He loved Moreta?' I was bold enough to ask.

Desdra nodded. 'When we collected the needlethorn. What a glorious day that was!' She sighed, the faintest of smiles touching her usually austere face. 'I'm glad they had that much. And perhaps, in a strange, unjust way, it is for the best. That is, if Ruatha is to endure.'

'Because Alessan must secure his Bloodline?' In all of Pern's history, no Weyrwoman had become a Lady Holder, though many Lady Holders had become Weyrwomen. Moreta had been nearly to the end of safe childbearing, but Alessan could have taken a wife as well. A Lord Holder could make his own laws within his Hold, especially to secure his Bloodline. Hold girls were raised with that precept firmly implanted in their brains and hearts.

'Oklina's children were to be fostered here,' Desdra said.

'But that's not enough with all his losses.'

'You must tell him who you are, Lady Nerilka.'

I shook my head even as I grasped firmly at the thought, at that utterly impossible possibility. He needed someone pretty and appealing, clever and charming, who could rouse him from all the grief he had endured.

She left me then, murmuring something about bringing food when it was ready. It took too much energy to tell her that I doubted I could choke anything down.

Chapter Ten

3.24.43–4.23.43

I'M NOT SURE how any of us got through the next few days. B'lerion stayed with Oklina. It was more obvious than ever to me that her destiny would be the Weyr. She had heard the outcry from the dragons, which was unusual enough for someone not of the Weyr or dragon-linked. Alessan's knowledge of Moreta's death was shatteringly unexpected to all but Desdra and Oklina. I pieced together some parts of their story, aided by a growing intuition that seemed to be sensitive to anything concerning Alessan.

All the dragonriders and most Weyrfolk had been instantly aware of the two deaths, Moreta's and Holth's. Later B'lerion told us of the reinforced rules and disciplines imposed on all riders to prevent a recurrence of this type of tragedy.

It had begun as a logical expedient for injured riders to ask their flightworthy dragons if they would fly a sound dragonman to make up Wing strength at Threadfall. Each dragon had his own peculiarities of flight that his impressed rider understood. But, generally speaking, any dragonrider was capable of riding another's dragon. No blame could be attached to Leri for adopting that custom and allowing Moreta to ride Holth in the several emergencies that had arisen. The courtesy was by then customary Weyr practice. But tired dragons and tired riders make mistakes, and that late afternoon Moreta and Holth had been pushed beyond mere exhaustion to the point where habit only had carried them through the motions of landing and taking off. I remembered then how Holth had gone *between* a wingspan above the Court that afternoon.

'Yes,' B'lerion said, his voice a broken whisper. 'Holth had lost a lot of natural spring in her hindquarters. She'd have leaped up and gone *between* before Moreta could have told her where to fly – they stayed, lost, *between*.'

Later, when Master Tirone began to write a celebratory ballad about Moreta's courageous ride, Desdra told me that, at the insistence of all Weyrleaders, Moreta was to be properly mounted on her own queen, not Holth. To broadcast the truth behind that tragedy could have done incalculable harm. Most of Pern never knew the truth. I'm not so certain I was all that glad to be in the minority. Not that it diminished Moreta's heroism in my estimation, but because so simple a mistake was causing so much anguish.

Desdra also told me, since she knew me to be discreet and trustworthy, how the dragonriders had managed to make so many deliveries. This had contributed to their total exhaustion, a major factor in the tragedy: dragons could go as easily *between* one time and another as one place to another. Moreta and Holth had overtaxed their strength in this way. For only by stretching time in this bizarre fashion or, rather, doubling back on themselves could Moreta and Holth manage to deliver serum to all the holds on the Keroon plains. Moreta had been the only one of the riders available that fateful day sufficiently familiar with Keroon's many half-hidden holds to have succeeded in that task.

Telgar Weyr was to suffer disciplinary action from the other Weyrs, led by Weyrwomen. They were unalterably convinced that, had M'tani not been so intransigent and permitted his riders to fly, Moreta's life would not have been lost. I never did learn what was done against Telgar Weyr. If Oklina ever knew, she never mentioned it.

I also was now in a far better way of understanding how the six people – Alessan, Moreta, Capiam, Desdra, Oklina and B'lerion – had spent that hour preceding my arrival at Ruatha. I had previously assumed that supplies of needlethorn had been available, not that these six courageous people had dared to spend a whole day in the future harvesting the thorns on far Ista.

I understood a great deal – yet it was not enough to help Alessan. I knew only that I wondered how he would find the courage to continue after this latest brutal tragedy.

He came back to consciousness, and awareness of this new sorrow, twenty-four hours later. I had been dozing, and roused at the slight sound his restlessness occasioned. I had to look away from his haunted, almost wild eyes.

'Desdra drugged me?' When I nodded, my own eyes downcast, he cursed her. 'It won't help. Nothing will help. Does anyone know what happened?'

So I told him, somehow able to keep my voice level and calm though my throat kept closing up. The waves of grief that rolled from the man were palpable. He stared at me when I had finished, eyes burning in his drained white face.

'But Leri and Orlith could go together!' His resentment and fury were compressed into that accusation.

'The eggs. Orlith stays until they hatch, Leri with her.'

'Brave Leri! Gallant Orlith!' His sarcasm made me flinch, but the agony in his rigid body, his clenched fists, told me that a different struggle was being fought. 'Dragons and riders have many advantages denied us! Would that my father had released me on that Search! When I consider how much different my life would have been. . . .' He turned away from me, his face towards the window. Then, because I knew his view included the burial mounds, I knew why he turned back, his shadowed eyes closed in the taut skin of his tormented face.

'So you have watched me while I slept, loyal Rill. And I shall have a new guardian, no doubt, whenever I wake, to keep me living a life I have no wish to live.'

My own anguish spoke then, not the sensible, patient, dutiful, plain member of the Fort Hold Horde, but Suriana's friend, Alessan's newest holder, and someone who valued him far more than she should. Any sorrow may be borne. Time will heal the deepest hurt of heart – but time must be won.

'You may not want to live, Lord Holder of Ruatha, but you don't have the right to die!'

'Ruatha is no longer sufficient reason for me to live!' he told me in a bitter, intense, angry voice. 'It's tried to kill me once already.'

'And you have fought to save it. No one else could have done so much, with so much honour and dignity.'

'Honour and dignity mean nothing in the grave!' He flung his arm up, towards the window and the graves of so many.

'You still breathe, and you are Ruatha.' I spoke sharply, wondering if anything I said could jolt him out of the course he had tacitly announced. Duty and honour and tradition were such cold substitutes for a beautiful woman and her love. 'As your holder, Lord Alessan, I require that you have an heir of your Blood to leave behind you.' I surprised myself with the vehemence in my voice, and he frowned as he looked up at me. 'Unless you want Fort or Tillek or Crom Blood to hold Ruatha at your defection. Then I'll mix the fellis for you myself and you can quit!'

'A bargain, then.' With a quickness I hadn't expected from a man lying abed so racked and spent with grief, he was upright, extending an implacable hand to me. 'When you are with child, Nerilka, I'll drink that cup.'

I stared back at him, aghast that my rallying words had evoked such a response from him, stunned that he misconstrued what I had said and applied it personally to me. Then I realized that he knew my name.

'Your parents have always favoured an alliance. . . .' His words were derisive, sneering.

'Not me, Alessan, not me.'

'Why not you, Nerilka? You've shown all the qualities of the perfectly trained Lady Holder. Why else are you so fortuitously at Ruatha? Or did you think to revenge those deaths on me?'

'Oh, no! No! I could no longer endure Fort. Tolocamp sank himself beneath contempt. How could I remain there when he denied the healers medicine and help? Coming here was chance. I was at Bestrum's when M'barak came and asked for help. How can you know who I am?'

'Suriana.' Then, more irritably, he said, 'You fostered with her, Rill. You know how endlessly she sketched. Your face appeared in many drawings. How could I not know Nerilka when we finally met? What I didn't know was why you'd come, so I let you have your anonymity.' Then he snapped his fingers impatiently. 'Come, girl, it is not so bad a bargain, to be undisputed Lady Holder of Ruatha, and no Lord to abuse you for ever. You can't be afraid of me? I never beat Suriana. Surely she told you that I was a good husband to her.'

She had told me that, not in so many words, but implying much more than goodness, but the thought of her now dead, and of his so palpable grief for Moreta, made the tears flow down my cheeks again.

'You are kind and good and brave, and do not deserve to be so ill used by circumstance.'

'I seem unable to avoid misfortunes, Nerilka.' His voice was harsh, his face coldly set. 'Spare me your pity. I have no use for it. Give me instead the child to carry on Ruathan Blood? And the cup?'

How I could have agreed to either part of the bizarre bargain I now wonder, but at the time I thought that surely when the worst of his grief had passed Alessan

118

would reconsider taking the cup even if I could find the courage to mix it. I would have said anything at that moment.

'Then let us begin the first now.' His hand compelled me to the bed, but I broke his grip, horrified, not entirely by his precipitous behaviour.

'No, I will not imitate Anella.'

Alessan regarded me with angry incomprehension.

'Tolocamp had Anella in his bed an hour after he knew my mother was dead.'

'Our circumstances are vastly different, Nerilka.' His expression was terrible, his eyes now burning.

'You loved Moreta.'

A muscle in his cheek twitched and his eyes stared coldly at me, glittering with something so akin to hatred that I recoiled.

'Is that what holds you back, Lady Nerilka? I'd liefer it be maidenly modesty. I never knew a Fortian to go back on his word.'

He taunted me and, exerting pressure on my hand, drew me inexorably to him. I tried to put in words any one of the many reasons why I resisted him then, the main of which was that this was such an inauspicious moment for a proceeding that was reputed to delight the participants.

'A man who has tasted death needs loving to remind him of life, Nerilka.' Now his voice was persuasive, and I was very close to capitulation when we both heard the scrape of the outer door and quiet footfalls.

'You are reprieved, Nerilka, but not for long,' he said in a swift, low, intense tone. 'We have made a bargain – Lord and holder – and it will be consummated, the sooner the better. I long for that cup.'

Tuero entered quietly, relief on his kind, long face when he saw that Alessan was awake and talking to me. 'Were you wanting anything, Alessan?'

'My clothes,' Alessan said, holding out his hand for them. I got clean ones from the press, and Tuero handed him his boots. He dressed quickly, then led us from his room.

If his appearance was a surprise to those in the Hall, his manner was even more of a shock. He collected Deefer, sent a fosterling for Dag, wanted to know where Oklina was, and did not question Desdra's continued presence when she and Oklina arrived together. But he turned sharply away when Oklina reached to embrace him, and sharply requested that Tuero and I join the others in his office. Then, in a low, controlled, but uninflected voice, he told us what must now be accomplished as quickly and as thoroughly as possible.

Everyone was so grateful to see him plunge into activity that no one but I knew that he was setting Ruatha Hold in order for his death. Not content with physical labour, he spent long hours at night with Tuero, sending out messages, some by drum but others in sealed letters conveyed by mounted messengers. I could hear the first – requests for brood mares for his stallions, requests for any holdless families with good reputations to apply to him. Some of the messages were reminders of marks owed Ruatha Hold; I saw those entries in the Records. He sent everyone able to walk or ride out to check on the condition of the empty holds, to tally what stock remained in the fields and in what condition, to discover what crops had been sown and their progress.

I, for one, found no joy in the work, coloured as it was by his cheerlessness and dispassionate industry. We had worked harder making the serum, but a strong and good spirit had imbued us then. Now there was no animation in any of us, as if Alessan's emotionlessness drained us as well. There was even scant satisfaction in seeing Ruatha refurbished and clean, every removable evidence of the epidemic cleared away. Oklina put spring flowering plants about the Hall, hoping to cheer us up. Some of them withered and died immediately, as if they, too, could not survive in this atmosphere. I worried constantly that what I had said to Alessan had been wrong, that I had brought about this fearful change in him by appearing to condone his desired suicide.

Ten days after Moreta's death, at our sombre evening meal, Alessan got to his feet, commanding our instant attention. He took a thin roll from his belt.

'Lord Tolocamp permits me to take his daughter, Lady Nerilka, as my wife,' he announced in his blunt, uninflected way.

Much later, I came across that roll, wedged in the back of a coffer. Tolocamp's actual words were: 'If she is there, take her. She is no longer kin of mine.' Alessan need not have spared my feelings; but it proved in yet another way that an essential goodness of spirit was imprisoned behind that emotionless façade.

That evening there was a ripple of surprise, but no one looked at me. Not even Tuero. Desdra had returned to the Healer Hall five days before.

'Lady Nerilka?' Oklina asked timidly, staring with wide eyes at her brother.

'The Ruathan Bloodline must continue,' Alessan went on, and then gave a mirthless snort. 'Rill agrees to that.'

Everyone looked at me then as I stared straight ahead.

'I remember now where I've seen you before,' Tuero began. He smiled, the first smile I had seen in the ten days. 'Lady Nerilka.' He rose, bowing to me amid the scattered gasps of surprise.

Oklina stared only one moment longer, and then she was around the table, her arms about me, crying and trying not to cry. 'Oh, Rill. Is it really you?'

'I have received permission from her Lord Holder. We have a harper present and sufficient witnesses, so the agreement can be formalized.'

'Surely not just like that?' Oklina protested, snapping her fingers.

I took her hand in mind, pressing it firmly. 'Just like this, Oklina.' With my eyes, I begged her not to protest. 'There is too much to be done to waste time, or marks that we don't have, on ceremony.'

121

She allowed herself to be persuaded, but her little face was troubled. For my sake, I know. So I stood up, and Alessan took me by the hand, and we faced the assembled. He took a gold marriage mark from his pouch and repeated the formal request that I become his Lady Holder and wife, mother of his issue and honoured before all others in Ruatha Hold. I took the mark – later I would see that it had been engraved with the day's date – and told him that I accepted the honour to become his Lady Holder and wife, though it was hard for me to add 'mother of his issue and honoured before all others'. But that was our bargain.

Oklina insisted on wine, the effervescent white of Lemos, so that all could toast our union. The traditional words were spoken by a harper who could not smile and had no new song to celebrate the occasion. The handshakes I received were firm, and one or two of the women were tearful, but it was a grim wedding day. Remembering that I was a bride, I managed to smile.

Tuero presented the Family Record for us to inscribe our names, my Bloodline and the date, then Alessan excused us.

He was kind, and very gentle, and it broke my heart to sense how mechanical he was about the business.

Not much else changed, for I would not be treated formally and remained Rill to everyone. Uncle Munchaun sent me the jewels I had left with him, along with a small but heavy chest of marks. These were my dower. He also told me what Tolocamp had said when he learned of my whereabouts: 'Ruatha Hold swallows all my women, and if Nerilka prefers Ruathan hospitality to mine this is the end of her as my daughter.'

Uncle told me this because he wanted me to hear it from him. But Uncle thought I had done exceedingly well for myself, and he wished me good fortune. I could have wished that good fortune were as visible as jewels and marks so I could display it to Alessan. Uncle added with great satisfaction that Anella had been infuriated by

122

the news, having been certain that I was hiding in a sulk somewhere in the Hold. Finally she had complained bitterly about my continued absence to Tolocamp, who, indeed, hadn't realized I was missing until that moment.

Holdless men, their families crowded into wheeled carts or drays, arrived in a fairly steady stream. Oklina and I fed them and let the women wash in the bathing-rooms, managing to establish certain standards and values about them. Tuero, Dag, Pol, Sal and Deefer would chat up the men over a cup of klah or a bowl of soup. Follen would give them a once-over for health and fitness. Strangely enough, it was often Fergal who would have the final telling word; and to whom Alessan listened most acutely. He gleaned information from the children that sometimes did not tally with what the adults had said. Always to our advantage.

We were fortunate enough to attract younger sons of lateral Bloodlines from Keroon, Telgar, Tillek and the High Reaches, so that the Hold once again filled its empty apartments and there were more capable supervisors. Craftsmen were sent, approved by Mastercraftsmen, with tools and supplies. Now, when I walked up the cot line to the beastholds, there were cheerful greetings from the settled, happy women, and children playing on the dancing square and in the meadows before lessons with Tuero. Gradually our subdued and sombre meals took on some semblance of relaxation and geniality. That lasted until we heard from M'barak, who frequently was on convey duty to Ruatha Hold, that the Hatching was imminent.

Then all of us were reminded of Moreta, Leri and Orlith – and Oklina. I was horribly reminded of my bargain with Alessan. It was too soon to know if his attention to me was successful: that was the only alleviating factor for the stress I was obliged to hide from everyone.

Though Alessan never spoke about the Impression, we had come to assume that Oklina would be permitted to take her place among the candidates for the queen egg. We all knew that B'lerion came on more visits than the tactful ones he made by way of the Court.

I was dumbfounded when Alessan asked me had I a gown suitable for the Hatching.

'You cannot want to go?'

'Want, no! But the Lord and Lady of Ruatha will not absent themselves from *this* Hatching. Oklina deserves our support!' The look on his face chided me that I could even for a moment consider any other course. He was grimy with travel, for he had ridden far to settle the new occupants of one of the pasture holds. 'Look through the chests in my mother's room. She always had fabrics put by. You're too tall to fit anything already made.' A shadow crossed his face, and he quickly went to bathe.

He came to me every night, kind and thorough, until the morning when we both knew I had not yet conceived. I cannot tell you how relieved I was, that feeling overpowering any sense of failure that I had not immediately conceived for him, for it meant he must live another month at least. I would have that much more of his company to remember. I could no longer deny to myself that Alessan had always been important to me from the moment he had married my dear Suriana, just as Ruatha had been the haven denied me, first, by the circumstance of her death, and then by my parents' arbitrary decision at Gathertime. Now he was vital to my heart and soul in a way that I never could have anticipated in the wildest flight of fancy. I treasured every casual touch; sometimes, in the night, I would feel his questing hand, as if to reassure his sleeping self that I was still there. I cherished each word he spoke of approval for my management, my suggestions. I stored them up, as others might hoard marks or harvests, to strengthen me in the famine of his absence.

I admit that as Oklina and I, along with two of the new women who professed some skill with their needles, sewed the dress out of the soft red fabric, I sewed with a lighter heart than I had had in recent days. Oklina had made her white candidate's shift quietly in her room in the evenings so as not to distress anyone. When we women sewed together, she began to chatter, giving me bits and pieces of Hold history, even anecdotes from Suriana's all-too-brief time here. She knew by now that it did not distress me to talk of my foster sister. Indeed, I welcomed the opportunity to mention my beloved friend. No one at Fort Hold had been the least interested in my fostering days, or in hearing about a girl whom none of them had met.

Gradually, I rediscovered pleasure in Ruatha, in building the new foundations, in welcoming new holders and settling them. We practised every economy, of which I contributed my own share by way of that chest of marks and the management I had learned from my lady mother. The Hold was desperately shy of many staple supplies, not only foodstuffs. The Healer Hall graciously reimbursed Ruatha for, I believe the accompanying note said, the labour and raw materials used in the serum.

Alessan ground his teeth, but altruism feeds and supplies no one. We didn't have to argue with him to accept the very modest income for what his honour had prompted him to do. Those marks allowed us to buy equipment, to commission ploughs, cart frames and wheels from the Mastersmith, and bare necessities from other Crafthalls. Every item supplied had to be credited against the individual holder's accounts with us. I spent as much time in the evenings on my Records now as Alessan did on his. We worked together in what became a companionable silence, broken when Oklina came in with the small supper meals. I saw occasional signs of his relaxing just a little. Then something, external or internal, would return him to that terrible, sad isolation.

Chapter Eleven

4.23.43

THE DRUMS WARNED US that riders were coming to collect us. B'lerion came for Oklina, bringing a magnificent fur cloak to protect her from the chill of *between*. Oklina, Alessan and I, all in fine new clothes, met him on the steps of the Hold as he formally requested Oklina in Search. With equal but emotionless and silent formality, Alessan nodded acceptance of the Search and placed Oklina's hand in B'lerion's.

I saw tears in the bronze rider's eyes, and then Oklina flung her arms about her brother's neck, sobbing. Alessan stiffly unwound her arms and almost pushed her at B'lerion. His face was stony as B'lerion wordlessly led Oklina away. I knew how hard it must have been for Alessan, and bowed my head against this fresh onslaught of despair.

A red-eyed M'barak arrived to escort us to Fort Weyr, and I quailed, knowing the reason for such tears. It was Alessan who showed me the courage to face the inevitable.

Hatchings are supposed to be joyous days, since Impression celebrates the beginning of brave new partnerships between dragons and men and women. How today's Impression at Fort Weyr could possibly contain any element of joy, I could not guess, And arriving at Fort Weyr was even more horrific. All the dragonriders were red-eyed, all the dragons a trifle grey-hued. All the guests were subdued, though not all of them knew that Leri and Orlith had gone *between* at dawn.

Despite the numbers of people arriving, despite their gay and festive garb, there was no conversation, no murmur of pleasantries as we all trudged across the Bowl and into the Hatching Ground. I hoped the sombre mood would not affect the dragonets, or have some other unforeseen adverse effect. I don't think I could have sustained another disappointment: I marvelled once more at Alessan's great strength of character and purpose.

So I held firm to the knowledge that, if we survived this ghastly day, I would have Alessan's company for another month. I had to hold on to positive matters. I had to hold on to dignity and honour to sustain me in this day of crisis. I had to remember that I was now Lady Holder of Ruatha Hold, one of the oldest Holds in Pern, and that our sister was a candidate for the queen egg. I had the right to be proud today. So I held myself tall and proud beside Alessan and wished with all my heart that his courage would be sufficient to see him through the day.

He was pale, I noticed in a quick sideways glance, but pride must have strengthened him, too. As we entered the Hatching Ground itself, he courteously took my arm. I was as glad for his support, for it was difficult to maintain any dignity while hot sands burned through the thin soles of my light shoes. Alessan led me to the tiers on the far left of the Ground. When we were seated, he kept his eyes studiously on the eggs, focusing in particular on the golden egg slightly apart from the others on a raised mound of sand.

I looked about me, because I could not look at the eggs or at Alessan. Master Capiam was there, blowing his nose fiercely, and the newly created Masterhealer, Desdra, sat beside him, looking sad, proud and anxious all at once. Desdra would not be returning to her former Hall, as had been her original intention on attaining her Mastery. She was remaining with Capiam, and I so hoped that meant what I thought it might.

Masterharper Tirone and a huge number of harpers of various ranks were just arriving, so I didn't miss the entrance of Tolocamp and the gaudily dressed little Anella. She looked over the tiers and then pulled Tolocamp off to one side, distancing herself from us, I'd no doubt. The other Weyrleaders and Weyrwomen filed in, though Falga limped badly crossing the sands. Someone behind me pointed out the Benden Lord and his lady and the major Lords Holder as they entered. That was the first time, I think, that I realized I now held equal rank with such famous folk. Ratoshigan entered by himself, as usual. Craftmasters and their ladies arrived, although I saw few visitors with the Telgar Badge; many were wearing Keroon's.

Then I heard the humming, which grew in excitement as the dragons, gripped by a sense of occasion, sang a welcome to the candidates. Sh'gall himself led in the four girls, then fussily motioned for the boys to walk on while he positioned the girls in front of the queen egg. Other eggs were beginning to rock, and the dragons' song became ecstatic. My heart began to lift, my pulses quickened. Oh, please, let it be Oklina! That would be the best sign there could be that our sorrows, Ruathan sorrows, were over.

She stood there so proudly, no more a shy, uncertain, slender girl, but a confident, dignified young lady. I had tears in my eyes. I had unconsciously clenched my hands into fists when I felt Alessan's hand unclasp one, his cold fingers lacing into mine.

One egg, just below us, began to rock strongly. Others were equally agitated, and I could hear people behind me make wagers as to which egg would crack first. I wouldn't have won; the egg below us broke and a moist dragon head appeared, crooning piteously as the

128

dragonet shook itself free of the shell. It was a bronze! A sigh of relief rose from every throat. It was a very good sign for a bronze to be the first to hatch. The little beast staggered directly towards a tallish boy with a shock of light brown hair. That was also a good sign, that the dragonet knew whom he wanted. The boy didn't quite believe it and looked in appeal to his neighbours. With a laugh, they gave him a push towards the lumbering dragonet. No longer resisting such good fortune, the boy ran to kneel in the sand before the little bronze and stroke his head.

Tears were streaming down my face now, and I was hardly the only one so affected. No one could fault me for such a display. I had not realized that I had bottled up so many tears inside. To cry was to release all sorts of ugly little pressures and tensions. Like walking out of a long, dark dream to a sun-filled day. Then I saw through the mist of tears, with Alessan holding my hand tightly, that a blue had found his chosen partner. The hum of the mature dragons was augmented by the crooning trill of the hatchlings and the excited exclamations of the newly chosen riders and their happy relatives in the tiers.

Suddenly everyone had eyes only for the queen egg, which was rocking violently. As Alessan's fingers crushed mine, I realized that he cared about the outcome of this far more than he would permit himself to hope – if only because expressing hope or love or care of anything must, in his lexicon, mean its loss. That flash of perception gave me the insight and knowledge to persevere in our relationship, and to understand the man who appeared to everyone else as undemonstrative and uncaring.

Then the egg gave three good wobbles and cracked neatly in half, the fragments falling away from the little queen who seemed to spring from the shards. Another positive omen!

Two girls wavered in their stance. I heard Alessan catch his breath, but I was filled with a strange and overpowering certainty which girl the little queen would choose. Quickly and with considerably more agility than the rest of the clutch had shown, the moistly gold queen made straight for Oklina. I didn't know that I had started to cling to Alessan, but his arm encircled me as Oklina lifted shining eyes, her gaze instinctively finding B'lerion.

'Her name is Hannath!' Oklina cried in a voice of exultation and amazement, her face so radiant that she was truly beautiful.

'Oh, Alessan! Alessan! Alessan!' I kept repeating, clinging to him, unwilling to express the tumultuous joy in my heart, but equally unable to suppress it even when I knew how painful this scene must be for him.

'She knew Oklina would Impress,' he said in a broken voice, staring down at Oklina's glowing face. I knew he was speaking of Moreta. 'She knew!' He clung to me then, his grip so fierce I could not breathe. I felt the anguish in his body, the pounding of his heart. Then his chest heaved in one massive sob, and he buried his face in my shoulder, sagging against me for the support I gladly gave him. Was this the reason I had been made so tall? We stood like that only a few moments, then parted, Alessan sinking to the seat and looking out across the sands. I know he saw nothing, for he made no sign when B'lerion and Oklina looked at us. I signalled them that we would follow. Then everyone else left.

The silence in the Hatching Ground was profound, the excitement outside in the Bowl muted by the great stone walls. Finally Alessan raised his head, gazing across the sands to the tiers on the other side. His manner had altered in a subtle way I could not then explain. It was as if he had let go, as perhaps he had at that moment of Impression for Oklina. Had he ended grief as she began a new life? Could he find a new life, too?

'I gave her back her Gather gown there.' His voice was a whisper I had to strain to hear. 'She gave me hope and help. I can never forget her, Rill.'

'None of us should, Alessan.'

He had not wept, though his eyes were red and his

face blotchy. He wiped my cheeks dry, as Uncle Munchaun often had. He didn't smile, but he didn't look so stonily hard of eye and mouth. He rose then and stepped to the next level down, holding up his hand to me.

'Today is Oklina's joy day. Nothing, not even old sorrow, should mar it. Nor, honourable Rill, will I require that cup of you.' We had started down the tiers and he was watching his steps, so he did not see how near I came to tears again with this new pressure of joy in my heart. 'There is too much to be done at Ruatha, now we have lost Oklina to the Weyr. I could not have stood in her way as my father did in mine. Now I am relieved that I did not. I had to come to Fort Weyr to understand that lives end, and lives begin.'

'Oh, Alessan.'

We were on the hot sands again, and since I didn't have to be on my dignity in front of a critical audience I grabbed his hand and began to run. I had to do something active with relief boiling about inside me. 'My feet are burning, and we mustn't be too tardy in our congratulations.'

With a noise that was almost a laugh, Alessan followed me out of the Hatching Ground and towards the festivities already begun in Fort Weyr's Bowl. Above us, outlined against the brilliant sky, dragons crowded every available perching space on the Rim. And the sun made a gold of every one of them.

Chapter Twelve

3.11.1553 Interval

As I CONCLUDE THIS NARRATIVE, there has been no Thread to blot out skies for five marvellous Turns. Few signs remain of what Ruatha endured, for the burial mounds have been levelled and their sites are all but invisible in the luxurious grass.

And change, the change from unrelenting Thread, has benefited all. Kamiana is Weyrwoman at Fort, and G'drel, a genial, heavy-set man originally of Telgar, is Weyrleader. His Dorianth flew Pelianth on her next mating flight. No one hears much of Wingleader Sh'gall these days, but G'drel and Kamiana are often visitors here, and G'drel constantly teases Alessan about his runner, Squealer. He's about the only one, save Fergal, who dares, even though Alessan is generally easier to approach on most matters.

B'lerion's Nabeth outmanoeuvred every bronze on Pern to fly Oklina's Hannath, not that anyone doubted the outcome of that flight. Her two sons now play with ours, for I have fulfilled the first half of my original bargain with Alessan five times: four strong sons and a daughter whom we have named Moreta. Alessan will not have me overbear, though I keep telling him that I am happiest pregnant and never suffer as others have from being in that condition.

He is even permitting himself to show affection to his children. At first he pretended total indifference, as if any tenderness would mark them as victims for disaster. To my delight, they have been incredibly healthy, less prone to catch the usual childhood maladies than any other children of the Hold, sturdily immune to cuts, bruises and breaks that often occur in childhood. Our daughter, Moreta – and Desdra has told me quite sincerely that she is the most beautiful child she ever saw, so it is not only this doting mother who so describes her – has provided the sun to thaw the coldness in her father. He could not help but adore her, for she seems to blossom with joy whenever she sees him, and her delight is contagious. Alessan will never be as carefree, blithe or gay as Suriana described him, but his smile is readier now, and he will laugh at Tuero's outrageous humour and smile at his sons' antics and boasts. He will cheer when Squealer wins yet another race and be a genial host when visitors are in the Hall.

We plan our first Gather, a very modest affair, when the spring has dressed the land with blossom and new growth. If occasionally, when we make our plans, a shadow crosses Alessan's face, it is to be expected, and I ignore it.

If he does not love me as he did Suriana or Moreta, still he loves me in ways he would not have known with his first wild and tempestuous wife and different from his deep devotion to Moreta. We understand each other well, often starting the same sentence simultaneously. Certainly we are of similar mind in every matter concerning Ruatha Hold and our children. He is public in his appreciation of my efforts, though he cannot know that his ready acknowledgement of my efforts is the greatest of compliments he could pay me, the girl who was never praised or thanked by her own Blood.

And gradually, as his fear of losing yet again that which is precious to him abates, his regard has extended to all areas of our life together. At night it is not the shadow of Suriana or the dream of Moreta that he holds in his arms and loves – it is Nerilka, his wife, the mother of his children, and the Lady of his Hold.

It is time to end a story that began in sorrow and ordeal and has ended in a deep and lasting happiness. May it be so for others.

THE COELURA

*This book is dedicated
with respect and affection
to my good neighbour
Maureen Beirne*

'IT IS YOUR EXALTED SIRE,' Trin told Lady Caissa in an apprehensive voice. The elderly dresser bobbed up and down with agitation. 'He is dressed for hunting but wishes a word with you.'

'Then, it can't be too serious,' Caissa replied, smiling to reassure the nervous woman. She threw an opaque wrap about her and strode through the veiled portal to her reception room.

Though her bare feet made little sound in the deep pile of the floor covering, the athletic figure of her sire whirled from his inspection of a tri-dimensional labyrinth table game into a hunter's stance.

Caissa smiled at his reflex and made the obeisance proper for the body-heir of Baythan, Minister Plenipotential of the Federated Sentient Planets to Demeathorn, fourth planet of the Star, Cepheus Two.

As Baythan straightened from his alert half-crouch, he fiddled unnecessarily with an armband of stun-darts – a sign to Caissa that her sire had more on his mind than hunting.

'You have, of course, heard that Cavernus Moneor has died. . . .' Baythan turned back to his scrutiny of the labyrinth.

139

'And his body-heir is already thinking of an heir-contract?' asked Caissa, accurately divining the reason for her sire's fidgets.

'As usual, daughter of my flesh, you are blunt to the point of discourtesy,' Baythan replied, regarding her with his notable air of censure.

'No discourtesy, noble sire, was intended.'

'None taken, I suppose. I ran a check on the new Cavernus' genetic patterns and find no significant recessives that might combine unfavourably with yours.'

Caissa gave her sire a long hard look.

'Cavernus Gustin may be genetically sound, my sire, but he is inept in the hunt to the point of cowardice and almost incoherent save for the formal phrases which have been dinned into what he uses for a brain. Even then, he's apt to come out with inappropriate replies. His haste is precipitous, his choice distasteful to me.'

'I have certain reasons' – and Baythan drew himself to his full height, a movement that displayed his superb physique and emphasized a naturally proud mien – 'which I cannot at this juncture reveal even to you, why an alliance with Cavernus Gustin would, in the not too distant future, be profoundly advantageous. I think I am correct in my belief that you would prefer to remain on Demeathorn rather than take up the star-hopping life your womb-mother prefers?'

'Have you been reassigned, sire?' asked Caissa, startled by Baythan's vagueness rather than by his recommendation.

'I have not been recalled – yet,' replied Baythan. Despite his bland expression, Caissa caught a hint of bitterness in his voice that she had rarely heard. 'There is – and I mention this in the strictest of secrecy' – and Baythan's urbane smile compounded Caissa's confusion – 'a possibility that I may satisfactorily complete the mission which first brought me to Demeathorn.'

'As your body-heir, may details of that mission now be imparted to me?' asked Caissa as indifferently as possible, though every ounce of her slender body tensed with expectation.

'When I have concluded my arrangements, yes. Both you and your womb-mother will know. Indeed, so shall the galaxy!' His voice had a ring of triumph long delayed. Then his tone changed to the lightly persuasive one that she had heard him use to much advantage, and she became wary. 'An heir-contract need last only long enough to produce a healthy child, daughter. Believe me, when I say' – and his tone became more urgent – 'that a small sacrifice today might reap unexpected rewards . . . tomorrow. However' – and Baythan's careless gesture of resignation told Caissa more graphically than any ardent argument how important this proposal was to him – 'it will be your decision, my heir.'

'I shall give the matter my careful consideration, my sire,' she said, bowing her head and making the submission obeisance with her right hand.

'You'd win this game by playing black to white's 4S,' he said, making the move on the labyrinth board and smiling at her with gentle condescension.

In a glance, she saw that Baythan was correct but, then, he was as accomplished a gamesmaster as he was a hunter.

'You have been a joy to me since your conception, daughter Caissa,' Baythan said, stepping forward and gripping her shoulders. He gave her an unexpected paternal kiss on her forehead.

'My sire,' she said in surprise, for demonstrations of affection were rare. This Cavernus contract must be exceedingly important. She bowed again, in the full display of filial acknowledgement, crossing her arms over her breasts, her fingertips touching the body-heir tattoo that entwined the base of her throat.

She remained in that position until she heard her father departing. Then she raised her head to see him, with a triumphant swagger to his shoulders, stride through the thick privacy-veil of her reception room.

141

She exhaled on a deep puzzled note and slowly walked to the air-cushioned lounger, settling into it with less than her customary grace.

Not much interrupted her sire, she reflected, when he had hunting on his programme. That he had gone so far as to check the genetic pattern of the new Cavernus emphasized his brief visit. Caissa knew very well that Baythan had rejected several exceptional intra-stellar contracts for her. Yet, search her mind as deep as she could for the reason behind this extraordinary recommendation, she could find no valid advantage to an heir-contract with the callow Cavernus Gustin.

Baythan's hint that he might culminate his Ministry on Demeathorn was even more startling. Whatever his mission was, it had drawn the High Lady Cinna of Aldebaran, Caissa's womb-mother, back to Demeathorn throughout Caissa's infancy and childhood. Ostensibly, the High Lady Cinna had contracted to oversee Caissa's early training and education.

Part of that training, which included intensive study of the involved contracts of FSP society – body-heir alliances, heir-contracts, host-child negotiations and other personal service treaties – suggested to Caissa that the heir-contract between her parents contained an undisclosed clause. Certainly the Lady Cinna had obliquely referred to contractual defaulters often enough in Baythan's presence.

The High Lady Cinna was governor-general of four of the wealthiest planets in the Federation yet she made time in the star-hopping life that she led to visit Caissa and Baythan, to whom she had inexplicably remained contractually bound.

True, Baythan had an immaculate lineage, descending from the earliest of space pioneers, an excellent genetic pattern with few recessives. He was a skilled diplomatist, fearless hunter, deft lover, had impeccable taste in mundane matters of dress, design and art and, Caissa thought with objective detachment, was the most handsome man on Demeathorn. She knew that highly placed women frequently made the journey to Demeathorn for the sole purpose of conceiving their body-heir with him. Caissa's womb-mother, in a moment of rare intimacy, had remarked that, had she known Baythan before she had entered her own heir-contract, she might have conceived her first child by him as well.

It had become expedient in the twenty-second century for the wealthy and important men and women of the Federated Sentient Planets to ensure that their riches or hereditary positions remained in a direct, and genetically pure, blood line, secured in the person of one healthy heir-designate. This heir had to be conceived naturally (by direct copulation) and be physically perfect at birth, surviving that event by at least three months, or the contract was considered void.

An intricate tattooed pattern of special inks that could not be duplicated ringed the neck of every body-heir, displayed as warning as well as defence. The child was inviolate and protected by the most stringent galactic laws and penalties, thereby eliminating blood feuds, kidnapping and the presumptive machinations of any greedy sibling of the same parent. Each man and woman had one body-heir, distinguished by the parent's tattoo. Of course, man or woman could produce additional children (the wealthy woman generally employing a host-mother) and provide for them as they wished, but the one body-heir enjoyed an incontestable position, zealously guarded, rigidly trained and especially instructed to increase the credit and holdings bequeathed to him or her. And to perpetuate the physical perfection which was as important a prerequisite for the moneyed, titled and intelligent as their credit balance.

Once Caissa's physical perfection and health had been duly attested and Baythan had declared her his official body-heir and ordered her tattoo, he had provided a substantial income for her from investments and businesses on nine other worlds where he had shrewdly

143

placed his own inherited capital during his various ministries for the Federated Planetary System. The High Lady Cinna had capriciously bestowed on her womb-daughter rich mineral rights from two planets and three moons.

Now twenty years old, Caissa knew that she should seriously consider supplying herself with an heir and, by custom, be guided by her sire's recommendations. Dutiful though she was to Baythan's few requests, Caissa could not in conscience consider any sort of alliance with the new Cavernus. Baythan had, however, invoked the recollection of a conversation and a subsequent painful incident with the High Lady Cinna six years ago, the day before Caissa's fourteenth-birthday celebration, the day that Caissa had ventured to raise the matter of the private clause.

'So that I may know how to set out the most advantageous contracts and alliances for myself, Lady Cinna,' Caissa had hastily explained as the Lady Cinna gave her an unexpectedly sharp appraisal.

'You must ask your noble sire about that clause.' A slight, sly smile curled the Lady Cinna's delicately tinted lips. 'He is in default and I have no wish to embarrass him.'

Since the High Lady Cinna took an outrageous pleasure in doing just that as frequently as she could, Caissa maintained a bland look of enquiry.

'Be certain, my pet, to ask for the attainable in any negotiations.' The Lady Cinna took up her hand mirror, checking her elaborate hairstyle – golden at this season of the year. 'I unwisely erred – one of my few misjudgments. I took the promise for the deed, based on past accomplishments. Oh, I'm positive that your sire meant well and I thought coelura well worth waiting for. . . .'

'Coelura?'

'Yes, coelura,' said Lady Cinna brusquely, adjusting a drape of the gossamer fabric that garbed her. 'What else do you think distinguished this wretched little planet with its senescent troglodytes? Surely *you've* been told of coelura? Ah!' – and the Lady Cinna exclaimed in arch comprehension. 'No one at all, then, has mentioned coelura in your presence?' Her brittle laugh had made Caissa quiver. 'I could well appreciate that certain data had been expunged from public information but, as your sire's body-heir, you ought to have been told.'

Immediately after Caissa had been dismissed from the Lady Cinna's presence, she had tried to remedy her ignorance. Data retrieval would give her no assistance until she obtained official clearance. That meant that there was information locked in the Blue City's memory banks. However, as she was also preparing for her fourteenth-birthday celebration at which she achieved certain privileges and responsibilites, the urgency of acquiring forbidden knowledge was overshadowed. The day after that fabulous occasion, the Lady Cinna requested the presence of Baythan and Caissa and announced that she would leave Demeathorn within the hour.

'I have had more than sufficient of the company in your two pitiful Triadic Cities, and certainly more than enough of the hunting and fishing which are evidently all this trivial planet can now boast,' she told Baythan with trenchant scorn. 'Until *you* can fulfil *your* part of *your* contract, I shall return to my duties and obligations on other, better-endowed worlds.'

She had held that scornful smile, subtly goading Baythan to protest her accusation of failure, but he had remained silent, grimly pale at her insult.

'And I suppose, failing all else, you will bequeath your quest to your heir' – and the High Lady turned indolently to smile with arch sympathy on her offspring – 'who will undoubtedly make a competent minister in your place, knowing the planet as well as she does and so sensibly conditioned for the existence here.'

With a final scathing glance at her mute listeners, she swept from the room in a froth of fragrant fabric. Her denunciation of Baythan made it impossible for Caissa,

145

unwilling to remind her sire of that distressing scene, to raise the questions of the unmentioned clause or coelura.

Caissa could, and had, invoked her new rights as a fourteen-year-old body-heir to the classified section of Blue City's Memorax.

'Coelura' – and the display printed reluctantly word by word instead of with paragraphic speed – 'a passive ovoid aerial life form once indigenous to the north-eastern group of islands known as the Oriolis group.'

Questioning 'Oriolis', a name Caissa had not previously heard though she knew Demeathorn quite well, provided more perplexity and less information. The Oriolii were interdicted by the Triadic Council. For the first time in her carefully tutored life, Caissa recognized that 'triad' meant three, and she knew only two cities on Demeathorn, the Blue and the Red. Blue and red are primary colours.

'Yellow Triad City' elicited the information that there had been a third City, now abandoned. It had served as a trade and export centre for a product no longer available. Yellow Triad City had been put on minimal care one hundred and twenty years ago. An update line informed Caissa that the ruins were now considered dangerous even for protected excursions.

Summoning a geographical display of Demeathorn's large, roughly triangular continent, Caissa regarded it thoughtfully. Blue Triad City was in the south-eastern corner, enjoying quite the best temperature on its plateau. Red Triad City was in a direct line of flight to the south-west, situated on the vast bluff that shoved into the western sea. If one considered an equilateral triangle, the upper tip would put the abandoned city precisely north, again in an elevated position, overlooking the scattering of islands that staggered northwards, presumably the interdicted Oriolis group.

Further queries, even using her father's private code, brought discouraging answers that were in their phrasing subtle evasions. No sporting animals, no facilities, inter-

146

diction by Red and Blue rulers for residents or visitors owing to extreme hazards and lack of rescue units.

Caissa made a rapid calculation which confirmed that the range of any of the rescue vehicles serving the sporting and fishing areas could reach the furthest-north island at a push, even if they had to rely on solar-charged batteries for a return flight. She could extract nothing further about coelura, which, in her mother's estimation, had distinguished Demeathorn and which once had generated the need for the third city. Even at fourteen, Caissa had deduced that much.

She had abandoned such fruitless research, though occasionally in the first few months she had tried alternative questions on the Memorax. Then she had begun to participate actively in the sporting life which absorbed her sire, and occupied the planet's inhabitants and the many visitors who came to enjoy hunting Demeathorn's canny, deadly and diverse predators.

The intervening six years had passed pleasantly enough for Caissa, and she acquired the status of 'quota hunter', no small achievement. She had a reputation as well as private wealth to pass on to her own body-heir. Now, mulling over her sire's request that she consider the new Cavernus, she wondered how that could be connected with Baythan's boast that he would, at long last, accomplish his mysterious mission and restore his contractual honour with the High Lady Cinna. Caissa would willingly have supported her sire in any effort to acquit himself with the High Lady, but marrying that insipid Cavernus was stretching the sire-bond very thin indeed.

Caissa rose to pace restlessly about the reception room, reviewing heir-contracts and intimacy requirements. 'A small sacrifice today might reap unexpected rewards,' Baythan had said. 'I took the promise for the deed,' Lady Cinna's high pure voice reminded her.

Although it had been six years ago that the High Lady had officially left Demeathorn, she had made sporadic and unannounced visits to the Blue Triadic City in which

147

Baythan and Caissa resided. Aware of the antagonism between her natural parents, Caissa noticed that these visits invariably occurred when her sire was protocologically unable to disappear on a hunt or some ministerial errand. Very privately, Caissa likened the Lady Cinna's attitude towards Baythan as similar to the sly, six-legged deadly nathus of Demeathorn's deep forests, a creature of immense patience for stalking its prey from the aerial advantage of the closely grown ferfa trees. Her father, on the other hand, reacted like a man caught in a labyrinth, trying to find the one way out to the sun.

Nor was Caissa immune to her womb-mother's verbal pricks and darts. These were mainly concerned with the lack of 'elegant or suitable' males to carry on the quintessential qualities of Caissa's historically illustrious heritage of governors, explorers spatial and scientific, male and female.

Though Baythan had full custody of his heir, Caissa could have requested permission to go anywhere in the galaxy that her private income, which was large, permitted. The Lady Cinna had, however, prejudiced herself in her natural daughter's estimation by humiliating the sire in the heir's presence. In the strict terms of contracts which Caissa had studied, as long as Baythan lived he could not be held in default of that unpublished clause. A strange condition, indeed, Caissa thought, if, as his heir, she would inherit the obligation.

But Caissa had not wished to travel from Demeathorn, certainly not in the exalted Lady Cinna's company, for she didn't much like the woman's ruthlessness, brittle ways and excessive devotion to bizarre fashions, often including body changes. If such practices were essential for social acceptance outside Demeathorn's system, Caissa preferred to stay with her father. Again, being candid, Caissa had lately become bored with a life totally devoted to days spent in hunting parties and evenings in parties discussing the days' hunts.

The previous spring, Caissa had been tempted to travel

148

to another system and had asked her sire's permission.

'Travel? You've just got back from a visit to Red City. Oh, you mean star travel!' Baythan had regarded his heir thoughtfully. 'She's been nagging at you, has she?'

'Not recently,' Caissa had truthfully replied.

'For all of me, you can go wherever you wish. Although the karnsore season is about to start. You haven't forgotten your wager with Rhondus of Rigel Four, have you?'

'Certainly not.'

Baythan had smiled as he gave her shoulder a paternal pat. 'Good girl. Then go *after* the karnsore season. Do you good. Get your quota hunter status on different worlds. It sharpens the instincts.'

During the excitement of that spectacular karnsore hunt and her triumph over Rhondus by three kills, Caissa forgot her half-formed resolve to travel. Rhondus had been a good loser, as befitted his rank, and had invited her to join him in a hunt on his native planet. As Rigel Four was in the Lady Cinna's sphere of dominance, Caissa had pleaded duties which kept her on Demeathorn and tactfully introduced Rhondus to a Caverna with short-term contracts on her mind.

Caissa had been very surprised when the next ministerial courier had brought her a cascade of magnificent, perfectly matched firegems. In a handwritten note, itself an unusual mark of favour for a womb-child who had disappointed her dam, the Lady Cinna advised Caissa to choose only a man who could out-hunt her.

Caissa had chosen to be amused by the sly insult. Now, with Baythan promoting an heir-contract with a Cavernus who only hunted in caverns well enough lit to take full advantage of photophobic prey or rode after the fleet but timid rerbok, the High Lady Cinna's taunt rankled.

Hunting? Baythan had been dressed for hunting and he had not suggested that she join him. Caissa was alarmed. That could mean that the new Cavernus was already in the Blue City, had approached Baythan per-

149

sonally and probably been encouraged by her sire for that unspecified reason of reward.

'Trin,' Caissa called out, running to her dressing-room as she stripped off her wrap, 'dress me quickly. The new Cavernus may be making a call.'

A fleeting look of surprise crossed the old dresser's face to be replaced instantly by the appropriately intent expression of the devoted personal servant.

As she was being suitably arrayed in semi-formal morning attire, Caissa found time to run a computer check on the new Cavernus' public credit and property, hoping to find something positive about the applicant. Exact figures were not available without special coding, but it was obvious that the Diolla Mines of Gustin's inheritance produced a steady profit, the domestic satisfaction of his tenants and free miners were excellent, and his assessed private wealth included valuable mining sites on two of Demeathorn's four moons and active drilling in domed compounds on three methane atmosphere planets in nearby systems. She could extract a fine endowment in an heir-contract – if she could only stomach the sire.

Trin had just finished winding green ocean stones into Caissa's long, naturally black, plaited hair when Gustin's arrival at her reception entrance was flashed on the screen of her inner chamber.

Depressing the release toggle, Caissa welcomed Gustin, keeping her words formal as she invited him to enter. He had come, she noticed as he stepped within range of the visuals in the reception room, properly garbed for someone wanting to negotiate an heir-contract. He carried a gift-casket.

Caissa let him wait, observing with inner satisfaction his nervous pace, the occasional twitch he gave to settle the drape of a tunic which did not hide the fact that his shoulders required some padding. He was a shade knock-kneed, and his calves in their ceremonial laces wanted more muscle before they'd display to advantage. Gustin was, as most young nobles, handsome of face and,

150

aside from those minor deficiencies of shoulder-breadth and leg, well proportioned. What did not match his appearance was his mind, Caissa thought with a sigh.

As she swept out to meet the suitor, Caissa reminded herself that her duty to her sire required her to consider his wishes, to remember that an heir-contract was limited to the conception, gestation and bearing of one live healthy child, and that her sire had intimated that a contract with a Cavernus right now would have a reward.

Exactly three-quarters of an hour later, Caissa, dressed for hunting, was making good speed in the fast lane of the Blue City's internal grav channels towards the perimeter hangar where she kept her speedster. She cursed under her breath, using the more pungent cavern miners' dialect to vent her fury.

Gustin, having misinterpreted Baythan's hurry to go hunting with ratification of his suit, had achieved new heights of fatuity. His initial greeting indicated to Caissa that he took it for granted that any woman would be delighted to gestate his body-hcir now that he was Cavernus. He had shoved the gift-casket at her, running on about the wealth and comfort of his home Cavern as though his familial estate was vastly superior to apartments in the Blue City. Caissa had tried, without success, to interrupt his catalogue of the benefits of instant promotion to Caverna. She had tried to point out that this was only an initial meeting, that nothing was by any means settled and no contract terms established. He even opened the casket himself, to show her bluestones, generally proffered for minor contracts; but, to compound that insult, the jewels had apparently been cut and polished by a rank apprentice and were set in poorly etched platinum.

The combination of obtuseness and presumption on his part made Caissa lose her temper. Restraining the urge to throw the paltry gift in his face, she had pushed the casket against his diaphragm with such vigour that

151

his hands came up in a protective gesture. She relinquished her hold so abruptly that he stumbled, trying not to drop the box. She then informed him in explicit terms that his manners would have put his humblest miner to shame, that he was pretentious, miserly, impertinent and ultimately the last man on Demeathorn with whom she would consider a contract of any sort, much less one requiring the intimacy of conceiving an heir.

She had left him standing, gape-mouthed, in the centre of the reception room, still clutching the casket to his midriff. She was no sooner past the inner door than she had triggered the holdfast. She called for Trin to bring her hunting gear, unfastening her formal clothes, stepping away from the fallen garments and into the ones Trin hurriedly tendered.

She reached the hangar level in record time, seething when she found her slim speedster blocked by other craft. One of the privileges of being the heir of a Minister Plenipotential was that Caissa ranked just below the Triadic heirs and above Cavernii. She also had more freedom to come and go from the Triadic Cities without undue interference by the Guardians. Out of courtesy she dialled her exit request through to Blue Guardian and then ordered hangar attendants to move the vehicles blocking hers. Inside the cabin of the fast vehicle, she contacted Blue City Control for clearance.

'Just going out for a spin,' she told the Guardian on duty. 'To watch my sire bring in his hunt.'

'Now that may not be so easy, Lady Caissa,' the Guardian began, surprise and concern flashing across his stolid countenance.

He was a nice old man, in his thirteenth decade, and had taught Caissa much about the dangers of inner and outer Demeathorn. A teaching, she thought now, that he might regret since she had so well displayed herself capable of handling most of the dangerous species on the planet – including the ones from which to retreat without

152

loss of dignity – that he could summon little reason to deny her egress. 'Your sire gave no specific directions for his hunt. . . .'

'Oh, that's all right, Guardian. . . .'

'Lady Caissa. . . .'

'Thank you, Guardian' – and she snapped off the channel.

He flashed an urgent request to speak with her again, but she was not in a mood to hear advice or admonition. She took a north-westerly route, low along the mountain ridges where transmissions would be jammed. She accelerated to the top speed of her vehicle so that the dangers of low-level flying exhilarated her and demanded total concentration. She was not a reckless driver by nature, but the distasteful interview with the fatuous Cavernus, her sire's unexpected recommendation of the contract and the well-remembered shafts of the High Lady Cinna all combined to cause Caissa to discard habit and, indeed, common sense.

Now and then her speedster flushed game with its side-shadow. Once or twice she changed direction to identify the creature. She had no heart for hunting, or for company. Then she wondered if she'd've done better to seek out some of the gay, effervescent, frivolous companions, either City or Cavern, and forget in laughter and society the doubts that plagued her.

She turned north again, to keep the coast range between herself and the Blue City transmissions. Her thoughts turned back continuously, not to the Cavernus Gustin, but to her father's hope of fulfilling his mission. Whatever it was. She tried to recall with whom her sire had lately been keeping company, with whom he'd been hunting, even what his catch had been, and she couldn't call up a single detail. When he'd say that his hunting had been good that day, she'd conventionally offer congratulations and let the matter drop. Baythan had never been braggart of head, horn or hatch. Now that she reviewed their infrequent recent exchanges, it was singu-

153

larly odd of Baythan not to have stated where or with whom he had hunted.

But, if Baythan were at the point of fulfilling his mission as well as his contract clause with the Lady Cinna, what did that have to do with hunting?

Suddenly she caught the sparkle and flash of manoeuvring aircraft in the west. She veered seawards, preventing casual observation of her vehicle. She skimmed the rough ocean, watching as huge amphibians launched themselves at her ship's shadow, flailing with fluke and tentacle. She adjusted her speedster's altitude, for she'd hunted these waters enough to know the dangers. When the coast curved slightly north-west, she continued straight. She wanted no chance encounter with hunters, and one of the best preserves of the nathus was just inland.

No 'reward' she could possibly imagine would be worth accepting physical intimacy with Gustin. On that point she was adamant. But, if an alliance with a Cavernus was advisable at this point in time, surely there must be another noble with whom she could form a short-term treaty. Must it necessarily, for Baythan's purposes, be an heir-contract?

Mentally she reviewed the list of Cavernii, most of whom she knew for they preferred smaller residences in either Blue or Red City to their spacious subterranean holdings. 'Home' did not, Caissa had been informed by one Caverna, apply to caverns: they could be made comfortable enough and suitably adapted to miners' and artisans' needs, but were not in the least 'home-like'. Caissa had found the enormous caverns which riddled Demeathorn's coastal mountains rather fascinating. Or, at least, the hunting in them. As living-quarters, she did indeed prefer the sweeping prospect from her windows in the upper levels of Blue City.

Triad city. And there were three. Whimsically, Caissa altered her course for that abandoned third city. She

154

might as well have some goal in her flight, preferably where she would be least expected. Yellow Triad City, ruins and all, beckoned.

A sudden drop and an ominous wobble in her speedster's flight brought her forcibly to attention. And she was in difficulties. For the first time in her life, she had failed to check the fuel-tanks, and the remaining supply would not take her much farther. The sun was too far west now for her to recharge her auxiliary solar batteries, though they contained enough to maintain shielding and life support within the speedster overnight.

She changed direction towards the distant shore and checked her position. She wasn't far from the Yellow City on a north heading but, if the place was abandoned, nocturnal predators would be abundant and dangerous. She checked for the proximity of habitable caverns, and the initial display gave her none. As the entire perimeter of the continent was a maze of caverns, she keyed an emergency override and, after a significant pause, the display informed her that she was headed for the Oriolii caverns which were interdicted. Well, she couldn't expect help from them with her speedster emblazoned with both Blue Triad and ministerial markings.

Caissa was annoyed with herself for failing to check her fuel reserves. Perhaps that was what the Guardian had tried to tell her when she switched him off. Not that she couldn't be safe enough in the speedster overnight: its plastisteel body was impervious to anything except ressor acid. Those creatures dwelt near mountain lakes, lurking in forests between forays into caverns. She need only find a suitably open rocky area, preferably away from dense vegetation in which a carnivore might secrete itself. In the morning, the sun would recharge the auxiliaries sufficiently for her to return to Blue City at a judicious speed.

The jagged rocks of the coastline were now visible. Nearer loomed rocky extrusions that must be off-shore islands. An extensive one appeared on her scope.

155

She opened a channel now to report her position to Blue City Tower and realized two problems: first, she was too far from any Triadic receiver to report on the power she had left; second, a faint emergency sequence disrupted the regular channel configuration. She tuned as finely as she could, but the sequence remained faint, not with the irregularity of distance but with lack of power. Swiftly she cut in the locator, and her concern deepened. The distress call emanated from a point not far to her right on the large island. She swung the speedster towards it, locking into the thread of sound and approaching as fast as she dared once she was over the island's forested and rough terrain.

She skipped over the rocky bastion, down into the valley it protected from the sea. A sun-struck dazzle caught her eye on the north-eastern end. Then she observed the swath cut from the tree-tops and climbing vines, though rapid growth had removed the seared vegetation. She slowed forward motion as she reached the valley's far side. Then she saw the crashed vehicle. It was of obsolete design, and she wondered how it had remained airborne at all. It had skidded across the first low ridge, losing its guidance vanes, and had dropped into a gully beyond the ridge, its nose half-buried in the inland rim of the island's bastion ring. Caissa wondered that anyone could have survived such a crash, but the emergency signal, faint though it was, argued that someone had.

This might be an island in the interdicted Oriolis group, but no one refused to answer a distress call.

Slowly she circled the ridge and gully and found, not far from the crash, a narrow ledge which would accommodate her speedster. Nothing could come at it from the bare rock on the island side and there was no cover at all on the cliff looming above.

She tapped out a contingency code for her speedster in case she encountered difficulties. The craft, once its batteries were charged in the morning, was programmed with her precise location and would return to Blue Triad on automatic if she did not reset it.

Caissa donned a tough coverall, prepared herself with hand and thigh weapons, emergency medical and food supplies, survival kit and pack.

Before she could close the canopy behind her, the sky above her head erupted into a flight of rainbows, spinning rather than flying. Round rainbows that sang a liquid and lovely welcome, for she couldn't construe that glorious sound into menace of any kind. Standing motionless, she whistled back at them, trying to reproduce several of the notes of the thousands sung at her. A hilarious response, delighted laughter, greeted her poor effort, and she laughed back in pure joy. Whatever the darting creatures were, they meant her no harm. They wheeled and veered and, Caissa thought, seemed to be urging her towards the eastern side of the ridge, away from the crash.

She felt compelled to follow them, their happy exultation overwhelming her original purpose in landing. They led her quickly to an unexpected break in the island's palisade. A section of the basalt had fallen from the escarpment, creating a steep slope down to the edge of a little lagoon where the larger boulders formed an uneven horn into the water. The sea was burnished bronze, with the palette of the setting sun marking out jutting tips of other basaltic debris beyond the sheltered beach.

The rainbow creatures deserted her abruptly. Then she saw them congregate by the edge of the lagoon, by the black boulders. To her astonishment she saw a man rise from the water and stare in her direction. She waved to reassure him, mildly astonished that he did not exhibit more enthusiasm at her arrival, however long overdue his rescue might be. She made additional broad gestures of friendship and aid that could not be misunderstood.

In doing so, she lost her footing on the slithery gap, slid unceremoniously and bruisingly down the slope to the beach. The rescuer rescued? She had regained her

157

feet and her composure when the man made his own way out of the water. He might not have seen her ignominious descent. Only then did she notice that his right arm was crooked and he dragged his right leg.

She was momentarily stunned, for physical injuries were quickly corrected and deformities simply unknown. She sternly reminded herself that he had been in a crash, had had no surgical treatment to mend injuries sustained weeks before and she must be discreet and tolerant.

Then the man whistled in an incredibly complex glissando. The voluble round aerial creatures smothered him in iridescent strands. In a matter of seconds, they flitted away and he was clad in the most gorgeous raiment she had ever seen, his unsightly injuries masked.

'Coelura, a passive ovoid aerial indigenous life form.' That hard-won data flashed through Caissa's mind. Coelura! The only thing that distinguished Demeathorn! Fashion was of major importance to the High Lady Cinna. She would have prized as invaluable the garment the man now wore.

Coelura, spinning iridescent garments, had been the product of the Yellow Triad City. And was coelura the reason the Oriolis had been expelled from the Triadic Cities? Why? Snippets of information began to mesh. She had assumed that coelura were no longer available. Could this island flock be all that remained? Was her sire's mission to rediscover coelura? With bitter certainty, Caissa knew that a coelura garment would satisfy that unfulfilled clause in Baythan's heir-contract with the High Lady Cinna.

Caissa was seized suddenly with an anguish so cruel and a rage so deep that she nearly burst into tears. Baythan had sounded so positive of success. If he knew of coelura, how *could* he put such joyous creatures in jeopardy to the fashion-hunger of the galaxy?

Coelura trilled her a reassurance which eased that stabbing, unfilial accusation. They swirled ecstatically about the man they had clothed in splendour. In splendour, and more, for now he was close enough for her to distinguish that other difference about him. Crippled he might be, walking slowly to disguise a halting stride, but in his face, handsome in feature, was a serenity, a self-awareness that she had never before observed in any of her acquaintance.

Some heretofore unexperienced compulsion caused her to extend her arms forward, palms up, in respectful greeting. She smiled, a smile as warm and genuine as his, totally unprompted by propriety or protocol.

'You survived that dreadful crash!' she said, wondering how anyone in his present state could be as happy as he.

'Barely,' he replied, indicating by a slight nod of his head the damaged side of his body.

'Your signal was so very faint that I despaired of finding anyone alive.'

'The signal, my lady, has been on for so long I had despaired of its being heard at all.'

He clasped her hands as equal to equal as naturally as if they had met under formal conditions. The faintest squeeze of his strong left hand emphasized the irony of his words.

'You didn't expect to be rescued at all?' Inadvertently her eyes went to his throat, which the high-necked gown covered.

'I am now found.'

Her ear caught the note in his voice that augured ill for those who had not searched until they found him. Or perhaps he was not, as she had assumed by his manner, a body-heir.

'I have been considering the construction of a boat to take me back to the mainland. My absence might precipitate matters. Would your vehicle possibly carry two?'

'Of course . . . but not now.'

'Oh?'

Caissa cleared her throat, aware of his amusement at her hesitation.

159

'I neglected to check my fuel-tanks before leaving Blue City' – and when he smiled kindly at such a lapse she went on purposefully: 'My own fault, but I had not intended to come so far and then heard your distress signal.'

'How far will the remainder of your fuel take you?' His expression became concerned, and the flowing blue-green of his robe turned grey.

'By tomorrow, when the solar batteries have charged, I can transport you anywhere you wish.'

'Even to interdicted territory?'

'Rescue missions are exempt.'

His smile deepened and his robe brightened, too.

'And how do you explain your overnight absence to the Blue City Guardians?'

'With any plausible story I care to concoct on my way back,' she replied with a shrug and a smile to belie a callous indifference to truth and authority. 'Do not worry on my account. I am only pleased to restore you.' She faltered then, feeling a blush suffuse her face as if she were an undisciplined adolescent, for she was not conducting his rescue in a proper way. 'I brought my medical kit,' she added, reaching for it.

'I'm long past the need, dear lady. The coelura eased my pain as they also sheltered and provided for me.'

Anguish again stabbed Caissa.

'Then they are coelura!'

'They are indeed!' The quality of his voice cooled and, though his face remained serene, she felt him grow stern and his gown rippled darker.

'I've only heard of coelura once,' she said, swallowing.

'Once is usually enough.' His sternness was disconcerting.

'What I heard did not lead me to suspect their existence or. . . .' And she glanced above her at the glorious spinning coelura who were murmuring lightly, but without alarm.

'What did you hear?' The man was polite if adamant.

160

Seized by a sudden whim, she replied, mimicking the voice of a computer: ' "Coelura, a passive ovoid aerial life form once indigenous to the north-eastern group of the islands known as the Oriolis group." That was all.'

'And "Oriolis"?' the man prompted.

' "Oriolii have been interdicted by the Triadic cities and no intercourse is permitted." '

'Yet you deviated from your course to answer a survivor signal in an interdicted area?'

'A survivor signal is not to be ignored from whatever source,' she replied with mock reproval.

The man laughed, an easy, hearty sound, unlike the artificial and socially acceptable sniggers of her society.

Suddenly the coelura massed together, uttering a trill that was a warning despite its melodiousness.

'Come, we must hurry,' said the man. 'The sun is setting. While the coelura are abroad, we are safe. Once the sun is set, they rest and nocturnal amphibians prowl this beach. I have a shelter, rude but sufficient, a short . . . hop . . . from here.'

'But there are reasons why . . .,' Caissa began, thinking unfilial thoughts about her sire's possible involvement in this man's accident. She was torn between a desire to detach herself completely and a deeper, burgeoning fear for the fate of the coelura if her sire's stratagems were successful.

'*There* are more urgent reasons why you will obey me,' said the man, pointing towards the undulating shapes that were speeding across the lagoon towards the shore. 'The prinas are wasting no time. They have our scent.'

Caissa required no further admonition as he took her hand and pulled her towards the thick vegetation just beyond the beach. Prinas were as fast on land as they were in the water.

'The coelura will mask our spoor. But we must hurry.'

'I thought coelura were passive,' she said, deftly pushing back the thick growth at her host's right side. Coelura

161

swirled behind them, their collective voice now almost menacing.

'You mustn't believe everything you see displayed, my lady. Coelura are generally the most obliging creatures in the world but they also recognize danger.'

Then they had reached his shelter, built against the base of the basaltic palisade. The sloping roof was only apparent because the flight of coelura settled on its outline. Caissa couldn't imagine what had been used in its construction.

The man stepped to an apparently seamless wall and pulled open a doorway. She quickly entered and, as he followed her, the entrance sealed itself.

'I would scarcely call this shelter rude,' Caissa said, staring about her appreciatively.

The single unexpectedly large room was decorated, if not furnished, in patterns that glowed of themselves. The rock of the back wall was covered with shimmering strands. Natural stone formations had been transformed into a long couch. Other rock extrusions served as shelving for bowls of fruit, a leaf-covered plate and gourds.

'This is a beautiful place.'

'And you naturally have been taught to appreciate beauty?'

She gave him a sharp look for the odd flatness in his voice.

'I have been so trained but' – and she gestured about her as the patterns of the very fabric of the room seemed to shift and flow subtly – 'but this transcends that overused word.'

' "Rude" or "beauty"?'

'You are rude,' she replied stiffly, 'who are clothed in beauty.'

He smiled then, as if he had been testing her, and his smile reached blue eyes accentuated by the greeny blue of his gown.

'My apologies. I have been long away from graciousness.'

162

'Living here?'

'Living alone. And here.'

The care with which he phrased that qualification did not escape her even if she did not comprehend the distinction.

'May I offer you juice, or water?' He was the easy, courteous host after that curious exchange. 'While the coelura supply my needs, the fare is primitive.' He gestured with his uninjured arm for her to seat herself on the long couch.

On the horns of her private dilemma, Caissa hesitated. To offer hospitality signified her host's good intentions: for her to accept bound her as well. If her suspicion about Baythan's ambition was correct, she might be in danger of violating that mutual trust.

'Not the sort of fare to which you are accustomed' – and his gaze turned mocking as his garb altered colour.

'It's not that, truly.' Suddenly Caissa wanted this man's good opinion more than she wished to violate the ethics of hospitality. 'I often eat from the land when I hunt.' To cover her confusion, she reached to a thigh pocket and withdrew the emergency rations. 'I have these to contribute to our meal. Perhaps a change to your diet.' She held the package tactfully towards his left hand.

Once more he laughed in his spontaneous and infectious manner and took her offering.

'I *have* lived alone too long, my lady.' He moved towards the shelves, taking down the fruit-bowl and placing it on the centre of the couch. 'Make yourself comfortable. That protective coverall is no longer necessary and it must be hot.'

Caissa was finding it so and, as the man unwrapped the rations and soaked the dehydrated portions in a small bowl, she took off the coverall and seated herself on the couch.

Having expected stone, she found the surface comfortably yielding. Curious, she touched the fabric covering. It was remarkably soft yet firm, and she found herself

stroking it as if it were the pelt of some creature domesti-
cated for tactility.

'Is this also coelura-spun?' she asked.

She sensed his sudden wariness and then noticed that
his eyes were on her throat and the body-heir tattoo.

'Ah, I had expected as much,' he said, unaccountably
relaxing. 'Your bearing is unmistakable.'

Offended, she started to rise, but he gave her a broad
mischievous grin and thrust a plate at her.

'You're not what I would have expected for one of
your status. Here, these are bark peelings which the
coelura collect for me. Exceedingly nutritious for one
who has had a trying day.' His eyes were kind and his
manner so conciliatory she could not remain resentful.

He positioned the rest of their meal beside the fruit
and gestured elegantly with his left hand for her to be
seated again.

'My name is Murell, my lady.'

'Mine is Caissa.'

They smiled at each other for the belatedness of that
formality as they sat down.

'And, yes, my lady Caissa, this is coelura-spun and
the shelter is coelura-fabricated. They sometimes use
extraneous materials in their constructions. There was a
time' – and his face lost its mobility – 'when men and
women paid enormous fortunes to Demeathorn for coelura spins. One sufficed for the lifetime of even the most
devotedly fashionable.'

Caissa bent her head as if to select food but she could
not look at Murell, thinking as she was of the studied
elegance of her mother's extensive, ever-changing wardrobe.

'Each coelura', Murell went on, unaware of her
internal conflict, 'has only so much thread in its lifespan.
They are willing creatures, eager to please those they
like. Unfortunately, they are pliant and amiable to almost
anyone. . . .'

'They don't like prinas. . . .'

164

'Prinas are natural predators, indigenous to this planet.' Murell spoke in a wry tone, and Caissa, dressed for hunting, knew all too well that man was the most insatiable predator of the galaxy.

'Coelura must reserve some thread with which to construct its mating-net, a net which was considered by the connoisseur to be more valuable than ordinary thread.'

Caissa saw the colour of his gown turning granitic and as cold as the tone of his voice. She dared not look at him, suppressing her own roiling anxieties, inexplicably convinced that he, or his coelura-spun gown, would sense her increasing fear. A fear that had more to do with the continued protection of coelura from her sire's plans than with betraying their presence to anyone.

'The Oriolis *left* the Triad to prevent coelura extinction?' she asked in the composed tone that only years of training could produce under this evening's circumstances.

'I have offered you hospitality, Caissa.' Murell's voice was unaccountably gentle as if he knew the direction her thoughts were taking.

'And I have accepted.' Despite all his discipline, Caissa could not suppress the anguish she experienced at her invidious situation. Suddenly the fabric under her began to wrap itself about her legs, but the ripple was reassuring, not aggressive. She stared down at the phenomenon of affectionate fabric.

'Stop that,' said Murell in an authoritative voice.

Startled, she looked up at him, but he was staring at the couch. His command was directed at the covering. The material resumed its former quiescence. Then Murell's eyes met hers.

'You are a body-heir, Caissa. We have shared hospitality. You have come to my rescue.' His quiet words reminded her of duty and tradition, of unwritten laws of conduct and exchange of life-debts.

'Coelura is at risk right now.' She tried to formulate a warning that would not violate her filial obligation.

165

'Coelura has been at risk and no longer is.' Murell stated this, so quietly vehement that she was bereft of all politic phrases. He touched her hand gently. 'Once you have put me back on the mainland, all will be well. Not to mince words, your fortuitous arrival will seal coelura's protection.'

Whatever she might have been tempted to say in as direct speech as he had used was drowned by a savage shrieking howl. The fabric of the shelter's outer wall was dented inwards by a large body. Caissa was on her feet in an instant, reaching for the weapons hanging from her discarded coverall.

'Don't worry,' Murell said, smiling at her alert reaction. 'The amphibian cannot pierce coelura-built walls.'

The creature attacked again, and Caissa positioned herself before Murell, knowing that his injuries made movement awkward.

'I really do appreciate your effort, my dear Caissa' – and Murell sounded oddly amused – 'but weapons are unnecessary.' He emitted a piercing whistle.

The creature outside snarled, more in pain than in anticipation. Murell repeated his whistle in a different and complex sequence. The sound was taken up all around them, the outer walls turning a brilliant purply red as if emanating heat, though Caissa felt no increase in the temperature of the room. The attacker's shrieks turned to agonized whines, and its noise dwindled as it put distance between itself and the source of its discomfort.

'Stop that,' Murell said, once more in that authoritative voice.

Caissa swung back to him, immeasurably offended, and then saw that he was once again addressing whimsical coelura. The full skirts of his robe, now a purplish blue, had managed to wrap around her leg and tugged her gently towards Murell.

She caught his eyes, and he gave her an embarrassed smile, snatching the fondling fold from her.

166

Caissa giggled. Her hands, which had tensed into flat defensive positions, went to her lips in a gesture reminiscent of her childhood. But the stresses of the last hour needed release, and she had never been given to tears. At the sound of her irrepressible mirth, Murell, too, relaxed, his rich chuckle breaking into full laughter as dignity was forgotten.

Afterwards, Caissa supposed that she had clung to Murell as the excess of amusement overtook them. Somehow, his injured arm was not awkward as he held her to him, nor did she object in any way to being in his arms. He was exactly the right height for her. She laid her head gratefully against his shoulder, which needed no padding. She felt his cheek resting easily against her head as the embrace was extended long past the need of mutual support.

This time, as the robe enveloped her, Murell did not protest. Then, in an abrupt motion, he released her, stepping back, the fabric in danger of being torn by his energetic retreat.

'My apologies, Caissa,' he said stiffly.

'No apologies are needed.' She held herself proud, hurt by his sudden rejection. But the hem of his gown reached towards her.

'Caissa' – and he seemed to be arguing against himself to judge by the action and the conflict of colour in his robe – 'whatever attraction you might have just felt for me, might be emotionally experiencing, is caused by proximity to coelura attuned to my needs. . . .' He broke off, his face and robe flushing with embarrassment.

'Well, coelura, and presumably you, have succeeded! You have made an honourable disclosure of intent. I am not averse to it. Now *do* something!'

'Not in this treacherous robe,' he cried and ducked from under its folds, though how he accomplished such a manoeuvre she didn't then understand. By the time his hands were removing her garments, the light in the shelter was dimming. She did see the narrow tattooed bands on

167

his neck as she willingly sank to the delicious abandon of the waiting coelura couch.

Sunlight suffused the shelter when Caissa awoke languidly the next day. Coelura trilled a reassurance as she sat up and the covering lapped itself caressingly about her. Murell was nowhere in sight, though the entrance stood wide open.

She dressed quickly, despite the initial problem of disengaging herself from the bedcover. She must leave! She must take Murell to the mainland. Then she must speed back to Blue Triad City, compose her confused thoughts and frustrated hopes, far away from the insidious and seductive atmosphere of coelura . . . and, sadly, from Murell whom she must also forget. No, she doubted that she would ever *forget* this brief alliance. It would serve as a standard against which to measure some other man. If such as Murell could be found, for he had been man enough for her!

Profoundly she regretted the pressures that must separate them so quickly. She regretted the diverse circumstances that would prevent any future encounter.

She had just scooped the coverall from the floor when shadows crossed the doorway. Coelura trilled, and their joy made her smile poignantly. Murell stood in the entrance, his grey-blue coelura now fitting tightly against his body. She knew before he spoke that he had been checking her speedster.

'The batteries are fully charged,' he said in a slow deep voice that showed the regret as much as his garment did. 'With that power and what you have in your fuel-tanks, you should reach the base of the Triangle.'

'Thank you, Murell,' she said, putting as much and as little meaning as she could in that trite phrase. Then quickly she walked past him into the sun-dappled forest.

As they climbed slowly up to her speedster, for the path the coelura had found for Murell wound in steep but

168

manageable gradients, the aerial rainbows encouraged them with trills and whistles. Their song seemed to be aimed at Caissa, trying to lighten her spirits. She wished that somehow there could be a more joyous conclusion for herself, Murell and Murell's faithful coelura. But they, above all, and he for whatever reason, must be protected by her silence.

Fortunately, he had to sit behind her in the speedster, there being but one pilot's seat. She concentrated on her flying and the directions he gave in a composed voice. She could feel his presence in every pore of her skin. She tried to discount this tremendous attraction for him to the coelura he wore but somehow. . . .

He gave her a heading due east of the island and then pointed out the shoreline features where she was to turn inland. She marked one hundred kilometres in silence until he asked her to reduce altitude. The landing-site was visible as a rock-lined square in the midst of tossing vegetation that pushed against rocky upthrusts of what had once been one of Demeathorn's myriad volcanoes. She landed. She released the doorlock. He covered her hand with his.

'Go safely, Caissa. Be well!' His deep voice was charged with emotion. He stepped down, with an awkwardness that now endeared her last vision of him.

It was then that she realized no coelura were in evidence, dancing about him. She couldn't question that. Lifting the speedster to leave Murell was the hardest task she had ever performed. She did catch a final glimpse of him ducking into the jungle, the colourlessness of his clothes reflecting his regret at leaving her more than the most polished phrase.

When she was well within range, she contacted Blue City Tower, a smooth explanation of malfunction ready for the Chief Guardian. He responded by advising her of heavy air traffic into Blue Triad City and that she must surrender manual operation within sixty kilometres of

169

the Tower. So she hadn't even been missed. She could easily have remained with Murell a few days. . . . She abruptly cancelled such thoughts. No one must ever suspect that she had been north-east or anywhere near the interdicted Oriolis shores.

Trin had missed her and been keenly worried, Caissa discovered when she finally reached her apartments through the crowded grav channels.

'What's going on, Trin?' Caissa demanded. 'No, I'm perfectly all right. I forgot to check my fuel-tanks yesterday and had to wait until the batteries recharged this morning. I was completely safe from harm. Now, what is causing such furore? Cavernii seem to be assembling here like nathus on mired rerbok.'

'Both Triads are in the Council Room, my lady,' Trin said, her eyes wide in her grey face. 'Not a whisper why. None whatever!'

'Both Triads in the Council Room?' Caissa recognized a meeting of premier significance. No secret had ever been extracted from that shielded chamber. Further, Red Ruler had been reputed mortally ill. Yet, if he were here in Blue City and so many Cavernii congregating, an executive decision was imminent. She shook with an apprehensive seizure as devastating as large fever. 'I'll change and see what I can learn from my sire.' She *had* to know what was happening from Baythan for Murell's and the coelura's sakes.

She hesitated as she unfastened the garment that Murell had touched. With reluctant hands, she stripped it off and watched Trin bundle the clothing aside. Caissa had herself well composed by the time Trin had dressed her appropriately.

The many-levelled Blue Tower was a massive ziggurat, its square base eight kilometres broad, its subterranean facilities even broader. The upper tiers with their fine, far views were reserved for ranking residents, but even the serving classes had windows. The public facilities included an enormous Hall off which lay the shielded

170

Council Room and the Rulers' private quarters and offices as well as an immense Function Room where the favoured could promenade, enjoying spectacular views of forest, cliff and sea. Amenities such as dining-alcoves for large or small parties, dancing and entertainment arenas were situated on levels adjacent to the Public Complex.

When Caissa reached the Function Room, it was crowded. She had never seen her languid peers so animated. She ought to have enjoyed that evening, for rumour and speculation raised conversations out of the platitudinous to the provocative and amusing. But she found herself falling into reveries of her encounter with Murell. She re-examined every nuance and word, every caress and glance. She couldn't concentrate on what anyone said to her, no matter how witty or outrageous. Nor could she find her sire among the milling horde of elegant people. Curiously enough, no one enquired from her of his health or whereabouts. She didn't at first notice that omission, being required to greet visiting Cavernii and parry their urgent queries as to the Council's extraordinary invocation. She even remembered to laugh as if she ought to know and couldn't tell. Finally, she gave up searching for Baythan, to find herself looking out to the north-east. Surely that was a coincidence, but she permitted herself to gaze long into the twilight distance, seeing but not seeing the lights of transports homing in on the Blue City Tower.

Then she had to admit that she might be just slightly infatuated by Murell. Although she'd experienced that sort of shallow lustfulness before, her thoughts of Murell dwelt less on the sensuality of that brief relationship and more on the concepts exchanged and her intense desire to see him just once more. While loving, they had continued to converse, silent only when their mutual need demanded satiation. But they had talked with rare candidness, in total empathy, one with the other, for that short night. How different Murell had been, mused

171

Caissa, sighing as she forced herself back to the social
exigencies of the company she now graced.

Then she saw her sire, making his way quickly towards
her through the crowds. He had a compliment for her
film-mist costume. The hazy dress was the nearest thing
in her wardrobe to coelura. Indeed, she ached within
her fashionable mist for the rare and personal touch of
coelura: Murell's coelura, a garment that fitted the wearer
as more than skin and soul!

'The Cavernus Gustin met you?' Baythan's expression
was politely attentive. Nor did his eyes betray more than
a casual interest in her answer.

'I met him, my sire, and rejected him as well as his
casket of badly cut bluestones!' Caissa allowed contempt
to seep into her formal words.

'Too bad,' said Baythan insincerely. 'Look about you,
my dear heir. The best and the worst are gathered.
Including some you may not have previously encountered.'

Caissa inclined her head. 'Was your hunt productive?'
she asked, feigning indifference to the answer.

'My hunting gave me great satisfaction.' The quiet note
in his voice, the slight raising of his chest, the tiniest
suspicion of a glint in his eyes told Caissa more than she
wanted to know.

'Oh?'

'Yes, my heir. Look for a Cavernus to please you –
just long enough to supply your need.'

He smoothly glided past her towards an important
Caverna and her escort. Caissa knew that Baythan had
told her all he intended her to know.

And she desperately needed to know more. She must
discover with whom he had hunted that previous day,
where he had been hunting lately. She questioned his
usual companions discreetly, but each thought Baythan
had hunted with someone else.

'He does hunt solitary sometimes, Caissa,' one frequent comrade told her. 'Says it's more sporting for the

172

prey if he's got no back-up. Reckless of him, but that's Baythan!'

She left the Function Room then and returned to her own quarters. With the basest and best of motives, she used her sire's code to check on his speedster. All flights were entered in the Blue Tower's air traffic control, but the log of Baythan's craft told her nothing. Distance travelled, mechanical servicing required, fuel used, but all his flights were entered for the hunting preserves. Which, as Caissa knew, did not indicate his actual destinations.

She wished she could ease her terrible fear that her sire had been hunting coelura. Though how he could she didn't understand. Murell had seemed to think that there had been no illegal visitations to the interdicted Oriolis. But, then, he had been wrecked on that island for weeks. Caissa reviewed her sire's interests during that period. She checked his daily log and appointments, and he had, as usual, been hunting. Unless he had to attend either the Blue or Red Ruler, Baythan had hunted some part of every day for years.

The next week was one of dreadful suspense for Caissa. Though Baythan did not permit her any private conversation, he watched her so intently that she had to affect interest in the various Cavernii to whom he introduced her and appear to be enjoying the festivities. Then it was announced that the privy negotiations of the two Rulers had been concluded. No more than that, but the atmosphere turned electric, a current of jubilation rather than of apprehension. Caissa's fear for the coelura mounted in direct proportion to the lack of more explicit detail.

On the eighth morning after her return to Blue City, Baythan presented himself at her quarters, dressed in the skin-fitting attire he customarily wore daytimes when not hunting.

'I am entering a contract with a Caverna,' he told her casually. Then smiled as he glanced down at the resolution of the labyrinth game. 'Well done, my dear

173

Caissa. As my body-heir, you will favour me by being present at the ceremonial signing. Rather a choice, if unexpected, contract for me,' he said, glancing at his reflection in the mirrors.

Caissa knew that she was expected to believe that his contract was spontaneous, but she did not. Too many ploys had been cast at her sire on Demeathorn for him to acquiesce so amiably during this past week. Her anxiety for the coelura intensified.

'An heir-contract is being entered,' he went on, more concerned about the small pucker across his lower back than about his body-heir's opinion. 'She's young and needs guidance for her heir' – and Baythan favoured Caissa with a doting smile. 'I shall expect you to make allowances for that. She's never resided in either city. Rather a good move on my part. Good hunting in her area. Brilliant, you might say. You'll know the whole of it soon enough, Caissa. Meanwhile, deny any rumours.'

'Of course, sire,' she managed to say through taut lips.

'You never disappoint me, Caissa. You are as discreet as stone.'

Caissa lowered her eyelids in acceptance of that barbed compliment.

'You would do well to follow my example and secure a Cavernus for yourself. There must be one man on Demeathorn you could endure for the time it takes to get an heir.'

With that, he gave her a formal leave-taking and strode out.

Caissa was shattered. What her father had not said, not even the name of the Caverna nor her area, confirmed suspicions that Baythan would have no way of knowing she entertained. Somehow her sire had encountered the Oriolis Caverna and persuaded the unsophisticated and sheltered girl to enter an heir-contract. And that heir-contract must include benefits and concessions which caused the two Rulers to meet in extraordinary council. Quite likely to remove the interdiction and sanctions on

174

Oriolis. Caissa comprehended with a sickness in her soul that was close to active nausea that one of those concessions would concern coelura. She trembled now with disgust that it was her sire's machinations that would endanger coelura.

Yet Murell had told her, several times, that coelura were safe. Had he not also indirectly hinted that the Oriolis isolation would soon end? But, if he were part of coeluran protection and had been deliberately abandoned on that island, had he walked into another trap?

She knew the co-ordinates of the landing-strip where she had left him. She stripped off her morning wear, dialling for her speedster to be fuelled and ready as she donned flying gear. She was dressed before her call got through to the hangar manager.

'I do apologize, Lady Caissa,' he said with proper deference, 'but no private vehicles are allowed clearance before—'

'You forget who I am!' Caissa did not often use rank on those in subordinate positions but she had to find Murell.

The manager stammered a repetition of his orders and added that these were issued by the Triad Rulers. Incoming traffic was thick as splodges, he said, and he didn't know where he was going to put them.

'Your problems don't interest me. I intend to hunt today!'

She disconnected, her finger trembling as she punched the Chief Guardian's code. After some delay, he greeted her, apologizing punctiliously, but he confirmed the restriction on outgoing traffic.

'The rule applies to everyone, Lady Caissa. We've never had so many people in the City and from some mighty unexpected—' His line cut off.

'Origins,' she murmured, finishing the Guardian's indiscreet remark. She clenched her hands until her nails made red crescents in her palms. How could she reach Murell if she couldn't leave the City?

She didn't necessarily need her own vehicle, she realized. Any one would do. In fact, the first one she could find with sufficient fuel near an exit.

She took the fast grav channel to the hangar level. Her rank got her past a nervous guard at a side-entrance. Gigantic as the city's storage space was, speedsters, cars, airbuses and even cargo vessels had had to be stacked to accommodate the numbers. The Oriolis vehicles were easily identified: their designs were so antique that she wondered how their patched and mended hulls had remained airborne. The largest one, which must have conveyed the Caverna, had been recently sprayed, and its canopy was so new that it must have been a pre-contract gift. There was no vehicle close to the exit that she would consider safe to appropriate.

Then it occurred to her that, if the Oriolis were here to celebrate the contract, perhaps one of them might know Murell. Three thin bands of red, yellow and blue had been his heir-tattoo. Too simple for much rank, she imagined, but enough for identification. He might even be here. She wanted to see him. She didn't dare to see him. Yet her sire had suggested she find a Cavernus. Surely the Oriolis had more than one.

Caissa was surprised to discover that the location of the Caverna's quarters and those of the visiting Oriolis was privileged information. Using her sire's code, she did obtain their level and direction. Surely, as she would shortly be in a contractual relationship, she would have access to the Caverna's rooms.

Triad guardroids ignored her request as well as her voiced demand. They'd been programmed for limited service and firmly recognized that limitation. Her name had not been included in their briefing.

Frustrated but undaunted, Caissa returned to her quarters. She changed into formal attire, for surely Oriolii would join those gathered in the Function Room for the evening's entertainments.

She wandered through the assemblage twice before

she realized there were no unknown faces and that her sire wasn't present. To her increasing dismay, she also overheard comment on all sides that, not only had the elusive Minister Baythan agreed to an heir-contract, but also the Triad Rulers were to make an announcement of planetary significance at the official signing of that document. Why hadn't she told Murell of her suspicions on that island? They had only been unsubstantiated suspicions then, the conclusions of privileged fact and coincidence. She would not really have dishonoured her relationship with her sire by voicing mere speculation. Or would she?

She almost cried out with relief when her call ring tightened on her finger, indicating a message for her. Murell? She found the nearest unit in the Function Hall and didn't know whether to be annoyed or relieved that Trin timorously but urgently requested her to return to her apartment for a moment.

As Trin had never before interrupted her attendance at a function, Caissa couldn't imagine what prompted the request, but any excuse to leave served Caissa well. She used the fast lane, reserved for persons of her rank or official android messengers, and might have missed the encounter had there been anyone else travelling at the moment. Something about the person in the slow channel opposite her caught her attention.

'Murell!'

Though he was dressed in plain service clothes and had his head averted, she knew a shock of recognition that couldn't be denied.

He glanced back as she swept by him, confirming her intuition.

'Murell! Wait!' she cried, skilfully turning and thrusting herself across the fast channel to catch him. 'Please wait! Grab hold. There's terrible danger for the coelura. Your accident might have been arranged. Please! Wait! Something has to be done!'

He had been half-across into the fast channel to evade

177

her when he paused, caught a handhold and pulled out of the stream to permit her to reach him. His face was as stern as it had been when she had admitted knowing of coelura. Since his clothing was dull as a servant's ought to be, and not coelura, she could not measure his real feelings.

'Murell, I only heard today. My sire is Baythan and has contracted with an Oriolis Caverna – with a body-heir clause for her, since I am his. And I wish I weren't, for he is somehow betraying the coelura to the Triad.' Did she just imagine that he was relenting towards her? 'The day I met you, he'd been hinting at achieving his mission here. It must involve coelura. He cannot realize what he is doing to those glorious creatures?' She began to weep with stress, her words tumbling through the sobs she tried to control. 'I tried to leave the city to warn you, but no one is permitted to leave. I went to the hangar, hoping . . . but I couldn't get a craft. Then I found where the Oriolis were quartered' – she had his unreserved attention now – 'but they are android-guarded and I wasn't coded for admittance despite the contract. I've been in the Function Room but there isn't a single Oriolis present. I did try, Murell. I did *try*! If there is any way in which I can help, let me know. The coelura must not be made to spin!'

Unexpectedly, Murell captured her in his free arm, and his voice soothingly repeated her name. He tilted her chin to make her look at him and then dried her tears as they drifted together in the backswirl of grav lap. She was astonished at his ministration and the kindness in his eyes.

'Be assured, Caissa, that the coelura are protected.'

'The Oriolii sanction the Caverna's contract?'

Murell smiled oddly at some point over her head. 'The benefits are manifold. The Oriolii may freely resume their position in the Triad. But I will avail myself of your offer' – he paused, bringing her hand to his lips – 'of support if it is needed?'

178

'For anything,' she cried fervently, clinging to his hands.

'We must part. Anyone could see us. Till tomorrow!'

He had pushed off, into the fast down lane, before she noticed the difference about him. His right forearm and leg were no longer bent in ill-set lines. She was relieved for his sake, but she would have been content to see him in any condition.

She continued on to her apartment, her body and heart alive with the joy of having seen Murell and delivered her warning. She refused to consider the niggling doubt that Baythan was a far more accomplished tactician than a Caverna who had been sheltered from galactic-scale contingencies. It was only as she entered her reception room that she realized Murell had said enough to reassure her but left much unexplained, especially his presence in Blue City.

Part of that was answered when Trin, with obsequious excitement, presented her with a shallow rectangular box of highly polished and unusually ornamented bluewood. As soon as Caissa took it, she knew what it must contain. Glancing at Trin's expectant face, she believed that Trin did, too.

'You did well to recall me, Trin.'

'The Lady Caissa will open the bluewood box?' Trin's question quavered with expectation.

Caissa would have preferred privacy to savour the thrill of coelura, but to deny Trin who had served her so long would have been ungracious, and uncharacteristic behaviour in herself.

As her fingers fumbled with the intricately carved fastening of the box, they triggered the lock's message.

'With this I discharge all debt.'

Caissa almost dropped the gift at the implacable tone of Murell's voice. Had she not chanced to see and speak with him, that message, piercing her heart as it did despite their meeting, would have compelled her in honour never to open the box.

179

Now she could and did. Within the bluewood lay coelura fabric, palely quiescent until she touched the folds.

'You must put it on immediately, Lady Caissa,' Trin said in an awed whisper. 'Only then will the spin live!' She stepped back to indicate that only Caissa could touch the length.

Caissa experienced ambivalent feelings of reluctance and desire for an acquisition that she had never anticipated. With shaking hands, she put the box down and lifted out the delicate length of coelura spin. She glanced questioningly at the old dresser.

'Wrap it about your body. It will fit itself,' said Trin.

Caissa obeyed, and suddenly the fabric was alive with shimmering colour, smoothly creeping across her breasts and shoulders, snuggling into her waist and down her hips to lap about her legs.

'Be ceremonial, Lady Caissa,' whispered Trin, her hands clasped tightly under her chin, her eyes enormous with delight in her grey face.

Regally, Caissa lifted her chin, squared her shoulders and pulled in her diaphragm, realizing for a fleeting miserable second that she copied that movement from her sire. Red spilled through the fabric, and it ceased to cling to her legs but fell in graceful drapes to the floor. Then the colour settled to echo the pattern of her heir-tattoo. Caissa, with an arrogant expression, moved across the floor in the haughty gliding pace that she had been trained to assume for the greater ceremonials. So she would walk tomorrow. And in this robe!

She could not maintain that cold imperiousness for long, not with the exultation she felt. Laughing uninhibitedly, she started to twirl in gladness, revelling in the comfort of the coelura against her bare skin. The fabric responded to her mood in pulsing reds and purples, shot with cerulean blues, breaking into spontaneous patterns as her steps fell into different dance modes. She exercised a hundred while Trin laughed and applauded until, exhausted by her excess, Caissa collapsed on her bed. Now the gown sobered and lovingly warmed her.

'You'd best sleep in it tonight, Lady Caissa, so that it knows you, or tomorrow. . . .' Trin's expression was solemn. 'If the Triads should learn that you've received a coelura robe. . . . Oh, I don't know what I should do, my lady!' Trin's hands pressed against her mouth in fear.

'No one will know, Trin. And they couldn't take it from me if they did know,' replied Caissa staunchly. She hugged herself, and coelura lapped protectingly over her forearms. 'They can never take it from me!'

'Yes, the gown would die with you, my lady, but I wouldn't want things to get that far,' cried Trin.

'How long have you known about coelura, Trin?' Caissa suddenly thought to ask.

'Oh, dressers like me, we've always known about coelura. I never thought to see it in my lifetime.' Trin shook her head slowly in wonder. 'Tomorrow, when your sire signs that contract, you'll outshine everyone else!' That prospect seemed to offer Trin tremendous satisfaction.

Caissa could not admit to sharing a similar anticipation. Since the occasion was her sire's, her attitude was unworthy.

'Tonight you sleep in the coelura, Lady Caissa,' Trin repeated. 'Tomorrow no one will know it's coelura unless you let 'em.'

Tomorrow, reflected Caissa, everyone will know about coelura. And someone will think to inform the High Lady Cinna. The irony that she should possess coelura before her womb-mother was doubled by the fact that a person like Lady Cinna was the greatest danger to coelura. Her robe gently compressed about Caissa's body, as if in sympathy as well as in understanding.

Murell had said, Caissa reminded herself firmly, that coelura would be protected. He had emphasized that. She only hoped that he knew what he was talking about. Did he, could he, appreciate how dangerous Baythan could be so close to a long-awaited fulfilment?

The exhaustion of the day's emotional stress overcame her. Despite her anxieties, or perhaps because she was enveloped in coelura, Caissa slept.

She woke, unexpectedly refreshed, her coelura a gentle green, a shade that illuminated her lovely complexion and complemented her black hair. Trin arrived with a tray of food and exclaimed with approval at her mistress's subtly enhanced beauty.

'You'd better eat well, my lady. It's going to be a long day and, with everything, you can't risk coming over faint from lack of food.' Nourishment was an answer-all for Trin. 'Coelura would give you away for certain if you aren't feeling well.'

The food did quieten the roiling in her stomach, and Caissa ate more than she intended. She did not like surrendering the gown even for bathing, and it clung lovingly to her hand until she, following Murell's example, told it to behave. She kept its dulled green length in sight as she submitted to Trin's ministrations. She sighed with relief when she could settle the coelura back about her shoulders.

'Now set it in your colours, Lady Caissa.'

She did, and Trin could find no fault in shade, shape or drape.

'You'll never want for the perfect gown again, my lady,' said Trin. 'It's only just too bad as you aren't the important contractee today in that robe. You'd have all eyes. No one would outshine you.'

'Outshining has never been my ambition, Trin, as well you know.'

'I know' – and Trin's deep sigh bordered insolent regret – 'but not for my want of trying. You shine now! I'll watch it all.' She activated the wall screen and tuned it to the Great Hall, now a lucent white as befitted the occasion.

Trin's excitement was nothing to the aura exuded by the invited and chosen as they moved towards the Great Hall in the slow grav stream, decorously, so as not to disarrange

182

their finery. The entry ways from all grav channels were lined with mirrors to permit last-minute adjustments before entering. Caissa's robe remained in immaculate folds about her as she stepped on to the platform. She moved politely forward in the press and pretended to touch up her hair as she glanced at the throng pausing or passing her. Everyone was, as usual, far too occupied in their own appearance to notice anything unusual about hers. She waited in the anteroom as long as she could, hoping to locate Murell. He might have chosen to dress in lower-caste neutrals to deliver her coelura yesterday but he did have an heir-tattoo. Surely he possessed rank enough to enter the Great Hall for the contracting of his Caverna.

The Great Hall was filling: the hour for the ceremony and the Triads' announcement near. Already the upper tiers were occupied by the ranking Cavernii and their body-heirs. Ambassadors and ministers from other planetary systems occupied booths and tanks or the balcony for oxygen-breathers. Caissa thought wryly that her sire was certainly going to achieve maximum dissemination of his new contract as well as his mission's success.

Although she had no part in the ceremony, she was his body-heir and would stand the usual three steps behind him, to his right. She moved across the immense Hall to take her position on the lowest of the four steps leading up to the two ceremonial chairs, red and blue, set for the Triad Rulers. There was, she noticed, sufficient room for a third chair on that dais.

With slow dignity, she viewed the assembled and, though she had often been a witness to prestigious contracts, she had never seen the Hall so crowded. Black guardroids kept open an aisle down which her sire would lead his new contract partner.

The sonic call-to-order peeled melodiously, through the Hall to the subtly carved domed ceiling. Before the last echo had died, two notes summoned the Rulers of the Blue and Red Triad cities. There should be three, thought Caissa rebelliously. For surely the Yellow City

183

would be reinstated and Demeathorn united in its original Triadic form.

She had always known that the two Rulers were old but suddenly she realized how old they must be, for unmistakably both wore coelura robes. She knew Blue Ruler to be in his fifteenth decade, and Red Ruler was older. Blue Ruler's gown was vibrant, sparkling; Red Ruler's blurred. She remembered the gossip that Red Ruler had not completely recovered from his recent illness. His robe, now that she had some grasp of the properties of coelura, gave strength to that report. Red Ruler's body-heir now took his place, and his garment, rich though it was, was a poor imitation of what his sire wore. He would need a coelura robe to maintain the dignity and authority of his office. How much compromise had been extracted from the obdurate Oriolii who had withstood sanctions for so long? Had the need for a new Ruler's robe been an advantage? And for whom?

Her robe began to shimmer and she hastily depressed her thoughts. The sonics trilled again, announcing the entrance of her sire and the Oriolis Caverna.

Simultaneously Caissa observed two things: firstly, her sire was wearing coelura that rippled in muddy colours, vibrating disappointment or suppressed anger. Secondly, his partner, as beautiful and graceful as a Caverna ought to be, was also in distress but she was maintaining the striped pattern of blue, red and yellow. Nothing in Baythan's noble bearing, his firm stride courteously shortened to match the Caverna's, would indicate that all was not as it should be. Then his clothing settled into a firmer pattern of his colours, but Caissa knew that Baythan, Minister Plenipotential, was under stress. Sufficient for his heir to realize that Baythan was not having everything his own way. Sufficient, Caissa hoped, not to notice his heir's costume was unusual.

Casual contracts, or those between lower ranks, were duly registered on the Memorax, but for persons of ministerial or cavernii status documents were handscribed

184

on a carefully treated paper which would instantly change colour if tampered with after the final signing.

Baythan's chief aide presented the large and beautifully detailed contract to the Blue Triadic Ruler, who made a show of reading before passing it to Red Ruler. Red Ruler's body-heir stepped forward and spoke to his sire. Red Ruler looked more closely at the document and rose to his feet, assisted by his heir.

'There is no mark', the old man said in a clear but forceless voice, 'or mention that this Contract has been approved by the Oriolis Cavernus.'

Baythan's robe streaked with grey, flushed to the red of embarrassment, though Baythan obviously controlled his private anger more quickly than he could his garment. The Caverna swayed, the blues and reds of her gown attacked by the yellow stripes, travelling from heart to hem.

'Gracious Rulers,' Baythan began, 'the Cavernus Murell. . . .'

'The Cavernus Murell is present!'

It was Caissa's turn to sway, but joy and surprise merely deepened the pattern of her coelura to a pulsing brilliance noticeable to all close to her. Baythan had whirled at Murell's carrying voice, instinctively supporting the Caverna with his left arm. Whether the girl had had any part in Murell's crash, Caissa would never know and later doubted. The Caverna collected herself quickly as she turned towards the aisle.

'I thought you dead, Murell!' Her voice rang with a relief and amazement which was, Caissa credited her by her robe, probably genuine. She would have rushed to the figure striding in the magnificence of coelura stripes, but Baythan's grasp recalled her to the proprieties.

'My profound apologies for this belated appearance, gracious Rulers.' And Murell made an obeisance, just proper for a Cavernus before a Ruler, yet something about his person – his robes – lent him an air and authority equal to that of the Triadic Rulers. 'My vehicle, doubtless owing to worn parts, crashed seven weeks ago and was so damaged that no signal indicated my position. When my injuries were sufficiently healed, I returned to my Cavern. I have but just learned of your gracious consent to reinstate the Oriolii.' Then he stepped beside the Caverna, who stared fixedly at him.

Red Ruler smartly extended the contract to Murell, who bowed before accepting it.

'That document is valid only if the Caverna is both Oriolis heir and body-heir,' said Red Ruler firmly, sternly glancing at Blue Ruler, who affected polite dismay.

Holding the paper by top and bottom, Murell appeared to study the paragraphs, his expression politely intent, but Caissa was positive that he had known its contents beforehand and had carefully timed his unexpected arrival.

'A minor addition will validate it since I am Cavernus and Oriolis body-heir.' Murell turned now and, for the first time, acknowledged the presence of Baythan with a very correct bow. 'I certainly have no wish to protest such a distinguished connection or deprive the Caverna of the wisdom and advice of your Excellency as her contractual partner, one so keenly interested in Oriolii welfare.

'However' – and Murell turned back to the two Rulers – 'as Cavernus and body-heir, rank and duty compel me to be First Comptroller in all matters pertaining to coelura spin.' There was a stir of suppressed excitement and shock in the audience. Murell bowed. 'You will find my administration impartial since I have no prejudice for those along the Base of the Triangle. It profits neither your two Cities nor Oriolii to continue an isolation for a cause that no longer exists. The species "coelura" are secure.'

Red and Blue Rulers leaned together across the gap between their chairs. Blue Ruler's shoulders were hunched with the urgency of the arguments he made to Red Ruler. Caissa spared a glance at her sire and saw that his colours were remarkably settled, his face composed. She admired his containment at what must be a severe check to his ambitions, for there was little doubt in Caissa's mind that Baythan intended, through the Caverna, to control coelura spins. He turned his head slightly, his lips moving in a phrase audible only to the Caverna. The girl blinked once, the only indication of surprise before her lips formed the negative. Baythan relaxed, and the slight tilt of satisfaction in the set of his shoulders made Caissa wonder what her sire's cunning mind had devised at this juncture.

The two Rulers had ended their conference and Red Ruler asked that the writer be summoned. Then he gestured to the assembled, giving permission for them to speak quietly among themselves.

Caissa could not quit her position and there was no one near enough with whom she could have conversed had she been of that mind. Except Murell. And she couldn't acknowledge him yet. Murell now came down the step to her sire. Baythan, with a gracious smile, extended his hand. As if released from a paralysis, the Caverna clutched at Murell's right arm with both hands, her face turned up to his, her lips moving rapidly, explaining many things as fast as she could. Murell covered her hands with his, his manner reassuring. Baythan exchanged a few more words with Murell, who regarded the Minister for a long moment. Caissa saw Murell ask one single quiet question and then her sire gestured towards her.

Caissa exerted every ounce of self-control to keep her gown from responding to the leap of emotion that surged through her. Murell inclined his head in her direction and then bowed formally to Baythan.

At this point, the writer, with assistants carrying his tall table and casket of writing implements, appeared from the Triadic offices. Baythan beckoned Caissa, his expression politely but earnestly entreating. She knew with a joy that did cause her robe to shimmer what her

187

sire wanted of her. She almost burst out laughing at the irony. Baythan would not find her so compliant if he tried to override Murell in the matter of coelura.

'Caissa, as my body-heir, I have the right to request you to consider your first contract to further our mutual interests.'

Caissa acknowledged that right.

'Would you consent to a contract with Cavernus Murell? I can assure you that the privileges of such a contract far outweigh any other that I have recommended to you.'

Caissa made the filial obeisance before she looked at Murell. She was very nearly undone by the twinkle of his eyes.

'What form of contract, my sire?'

'With so much at issue, Baythan,' said Murell, 'I must insist on a body contract of five standard years to ensure the health of that heir.'

Baythan was visibly startled. Caissa knew that he must be rapidly assessing the value of this double commitment to the Oriolii, whether it would improve or hamper his own designs and whether he dared insist that Caissa approve such a long heir-contract.

'Sire Baythan,' said Caissa, drawling. She pretended to study Murell's face and figure with a calculating eye. 'I should be an undutiful heir not to do everything in my power to support you at this moment.' But her eyes sought Murell's as she spoke.

The fingers of her sire's right hand twitched briefly in recognition of her unexpected capitulation. Baythan gave Caissa a sudden searching look of suspicion before he, too, smiled with every evidence of pride in her filial submission. He took a step forward to get the attention of the two Rulers, approaching to make his request. Caissa, who dared not look at Murell when her heart was singing as loudly as coelura, watched the faces of the Rulers. She thought that Red Ruler smiled as he listened to Baythan.

'You wear coelura,' whispered the Caverna to Caissa in the accomplished voiceless way of their rank.

'A life-debt, my lady,' Caissa replied and smiled at the girl who would now be in a double relationship to her.

The Caverna's eyebrows puckered slightly in perplexity.

'When I whistled coelura to spin two lengths, I thought one was to fulfil a contract debt.'

Both girls heard Murell's chuckle.

'No, a life-debt, Anvral,' said Murell.

'*You* rescued Murell.' Anvral shot a look of gratitude to Caissa and then one of anger to the Cavernus. 'Why didn't you let me know?'

'After my "accident", discretion seemed the wiser course. You were proceeding very well, Anvral, without my assistance.' Murell's eyes gleamed with friendly malice.

Then Baythan raised his hands for silence. He announced the double contract. As the Great Hall buzzed with agitation, Murell was beckoned forward. The two Rulers, Murell and Baythan watched the writer amend the document.

'How did you meet Baythan?' Caissa had a few questions of her own.

'*He* rescued *me*', said Anvral, her eyes crinkling with laughter though she kept her face composed, 'from an amphibian when I was searching for Murell. Are rescue missions to interdicted areas a genetic trait in your line?'

'My sire is known to be fortunate,' Caissa replied with discreet sincerity. This girl was not as unsophisticated as Baythan had been led to believe.

'Caverna Anvral,' said Blue Ruler, 'body-heir Lady Caissa, your signatures are required.'

'I would like to scan the document first,' said Caissa as she approached the writing-table.

'A wise lady,' said Red Ruler with a hint of a smile tugging at his sad lips.

Caissa knew enough about such contracts to flick

189

through the first paragraphs about obligation, responsibility, damages and sanctions applicable if the obligations were not fulfilled. The paragraph concerning her sire and Anvral gave two years of body-heir provision. In small but quite legible script, the writer had added the conditions stipulated by Murell.

The third paragraph she read slowly, for it outlined the end of the interdiction of the Oriolii and stated that coelura fabric would again be available for export and at a price per spin that made Caissa's eyes widen. Murell's name had been substituted for Anvral's as Comptroller. Official garments would be supplied to ranking Cavernii (so that had been Baythan's reason for her to contract), Triadic Rulers and their body-heirs at need and at no expense. Yellow Triad City was to be restored, an enormous credit balance advanced to replenish and refurbish Oriolii Caverns and surface facilities. Yellow Triad Ruler was to be nominated by the Oriolis Cavernii, that candidate to be accepted by Red and Blue Rulers. The writer had added only one line to this clause: the supply of coelura fabric would not exceed one spin per adult coelura in any Demeathorn year.

Caissa raised her eyes in appeal to Murell, for she could not see how such a restriction could be enforced. Surely there would be attempts to capture the beautiful and friendly creatures and remove them from Demeathorn, after which they could be forced to spin themselves to death. Murell returned her gaze serenely. In soft caress, her gown hugged closer to her body and she understood that to be reassurance.

She signed above her scribed name, handing the pen to Anvral. Murell affixed his signature beside hers as Baythan put his next to Anvral's. Both Rulers signed, and Red Ruler held the document high.

'We pronounce this double contract valid and inviolable,' he said, his voice issuing firmly, 'honourably to be discharged by Cavernus Murell and Lady Caissa, and by Caverna Anvral and His Excellency, Baythan.' He

190

motioned to the newly contracted to join hands. 'Let us now celebrate the glad occasion of a reunited continent and an equilateral triangle.'

Cheering followed as the two Rulers retired to their offices. The massive stairway to the Function Room on the upper level began to open, stirring the audience to rearrange themselves and ascend.

Caissa turned anxiously to Murell.

'No fears, Caissa. Coelura are safe.' Murell smiled warmly down at her and pressed her hands together in his. 'Both Anvral and I have been as carefully trained for this transaction as the coelura. Over the past one hundred and twenty years, the coelura have been conditioned to respond only to a certain combination of notes known to a trusted minority. With myself as Comptroller and Anvral committed to Baythan. . . .' Murell glanced over Caissa's shoulder towards Anvral and her sire when his grasp tightened on her fingers. The quality of his smile altered. 'So this is the other contract spin,' he said and abruptly swung Caissa towards the milling guests.

Caissa could not suppress her gasp of amazement at the sight of the High Lady Cinna, gliding ruthlessly towards them. Even in a stunning gathering of the ultra-fashionable, Lady Cinna was outstandingly garbed, her costume composed of the highly prized and costly imbia shells of a nascent gold. Her hair, dyed a subtly darker shade, had been dressed in long thin plaits, studded with tinier shells. The effect was dazzling until she neared the newly contracted couples.

'My sincerest congratulations, Minister Baythan,' she said in her most brittle and indolent voice, more like the sly nathus than ever. 'Quite a coup, in fact. I presume you have not forgotten. . . .'

Caissa caught her breath, swallowing down a taste of bile at the thought of the High Lady Cinna swathed in coelura.

'How could one forget you, Lady Cinna!' exclaimed Baythan, his voice as smoothly composed as the colours of his robe. Somehow a bluewood box appeared in his hand. He spared a sideways look at Caissa, and she must have imagined that her sire winked. 'A small token by which to remember sire and heir.'

'May it become you,' Caissa added, stepping with Murell to Baythan's right.

In a daze, Lady Cinna's hands closed about the box. Her expression turned from smug anticipation to irate dismay as she appraised the vibrant gowns which dulled her magnificence to insipid beige.

Her eyes narrowed with fury, and frustration pulled lines in her face which discipline and surgery had long disguised. The imbia shells shook with her suppressed rage.

'Honour being satisfied, my heir, let us celebrate,' said Baythan, bowing formally to the motionless High Lady and escorting Anvral towards the festivities.

Murell led Caissa away, the drape of their gowns enmeshing as his fingers pressed hers with the promise of renewing their first encounter.

'Lady Cinna really deserves coelura,' Murell remarked with droll humour in his deep voice. 'It *will* become her, you know!'